WALKING SHADOWS

DAVID BARRY

This edition published in 2018 by Mascot Press
contact.mascotpress@gmail.com

For Kevin at Channel Radio

One

As she listened to her husband rummaging around in his study – his 'sanctum' as he called it – her ears straining for the sound of anything untoward, Karen suspected she was being paranoid. Only three months after marrying him, she discovered she no longer trusted him, and she felt guilty for the suspicious thoughts which bombarded her brain like hailstone showers. She tried to clear her mind of the doubts and reservations which grew daily like an unhealthy growth, and every time he smiled that charming smile of his, instead of being reassured she felt nagging doubts stirring inside her. There was never anything specific, no apparent reason for her sudden scepticism, so she tried to analyse her feelings, asking herself over and over why it was she had such misgivings about their relationship.

'Is something wrong, Karen?'

She jumped. She hadn't heard him entering the kitchen and wondered why she felt so unnerved. Perhaps it was simply because he had startled her. As she turned to look at him framed in the doorway, and saw the way his eyes lit up, and his sensuous smile, she tried to convince herself that she was foolish to doubt him. After all, he had never given her any reason to question his sincerity or truthfulness. Always attentive and charming, during their time together he had never once quarrelled with her. No, that wasn't quite true. There was that one time when she went into his study to tidy, and he flipped. Overreacted. She had never seen him respond so violently before and it frightened her. Fists clenched, as if he was about to hit her, and snarling angrily, he screamed about needing his own private space and she was never to tidy or clean in there again. His eyes, she remembered, burned like white coals and spewed sudden hatred, and she saw another side to him. But then, seeing her weeping and choking from fear, he switched on that wonderful smile of his, held her tight and begged her to accept his deepest apology. After she had calmed down, he insisted she must leave his study alone. His own space, he emphasised. And she had thought no more about it, reasoning that the study was his male preserve, and it was territorial instinct which made him react in such a way.

'*Is* something wrong, Karen?' he repeated. 'You've been so quiet lately.'

1

She managed a tiny smile and said, 'Sorry, Paul. I suppose I was just thinking about Mummy again.'

He came towards her, waving his passport before sliding it into the inside pocket of his three-piece Hugo Boss suit, and it struck her that this was a demonstration for her benefit, revealing his intention of travelling abroad, even though she had seen no travel documents. He slid his arms around her waist and pulled her to him. He smelled of Paco Rabanne aftershave, his cheeks were shiny and she knew he had taken a long time over his shaving, as he often did when he had a business meeting. He stared closely at her, just inches away from her face, studying the anxiety in her eyes like a scientist examining a specimen.

'I'm sorry, sweetheart. I should have realised you're worried about her. How long d'you think she's –' He stopped himself from mentioning the inevitable.

She sighed before replying. 'I don't know. The doctor said it could be just a matter of months – weeks, even. That's why I wish you didn't have to go away – especially now.'

'I don't have a choice, sweetheart. This is an important deal. And life must go on.' He saw the hurt in her eyes and added, 'I'll only be gone for three nights. I'm sure nothing will happen in the next few days.'

She pictured the family gathered around her mother's sick bed, waiting for her end, like a scene from a sentimental movie. A weepie. And she guessed her mother would be praying in her dying moments for a reconciliation between her and Vanessa, the twin sister she had barely spoken to for more than five years, other than polite and awkward acknowledgements. Most twins, Karen supposed, were usually very close and forgiving, but then she and Vanessa were non-identical twins and had never had much in common. They didn't even look as if they were related.

Paul pulled away from her – rather abruptly she thought – and she wondered if he was irritated by the impending tragedy of her mother's terminal cancer. The image of the family tableau gathered around the deathbed in peaceful harmony vanished as she saw him glance at his watch, determination setting in to his jawline.

'What time's your flight?' she asked.

'Jesus! I'd better get a move on. I'm already behind.'

She watched as he rubbed a hand along the natural stone of the island work surface in the centre of the kitchen, checking to see if it was perfectly smooth, not a crumb to ruin its texture, and she thought about his

2

fastidiousness, the way he always wanted everything to be in perfect condition, clean and ridiculously tidy. A magazine must always be returned to the leather rack after reading, never left on the coffee table. Once, not long after they were married, he claimed one of the pictures on a wall wasn't straight, even though she couldn't see the tiniest tilt to one side. She was astounded when he went into his study and returned with a small spirit level to gauge the slant of the picture, which couldn't have been more than a centimetre or two lower on one side. And he was just as scrupulous about his personal hygiene, and spent ages in the bathroom grooming himself. Karen often wondered when he would begin dying the few grey hairs at the side of his head; or did he cherish the mature distinguished appearance it gave him, creating a robust businessman image? His visits to an expensive hairdresser were frequent, keeping his dark brown hair just the right length, never too long or too short. The only thing which stopped him being conventionally handsome was his slightly upturned, almost feminine, nose. He claimed he was in his mid-thirties, although she suspected he lied about his age. But even if, as she guessed, he had reached the big four-oh, she was nearly twenty-eight, so that would make an acceptable gap of twelve years. And don't many people lie about their age? So, that had never been an issue to lose any sleep over.

Satisfied the work surface was pristine, Paul wiped his hands, brushing off an imaginary blemish, nodded with satisfaction, then hurried into the living room. Karen followed him, saw him patting his pockets to check he had everything he needed, then kissed him hurriedly on his cheek. 'You will drive carefully, won't you, Paul?'

He chuckled audaciously and shrugged. 'I always do.'

'Since when?'

'Since I bought the new BMW.'

And there it was again, the doubts sending her signals, like flashing neon messages. How could he afford to live like this? Such extravagance and recklessness for a travel agent with only one shop – in Hounslow of all places. Yet they lived in an expensive area, a large three-bedroom flat in a purpose-built block just off Kingston Hill, so the mortgage payments must be crippling. And still Paul managed to live extravagantly: expensive restaurants, the best seats for arena concerts and comedians, designer clothes. In fact, designer everything. Only the best for Paul. Nothing else would do. And whenever she questioned his extravagance, he always made a joke of it; told her not to worry her pretty-little head about it. Most women would have been incensed by this, but not Karen, who had been brought up to never question her father's finances or how he made his money. On reflection, she thought, her father and her husband were practically from the same mould. With one exception. Her father was far more astute than Paul, and was careful about the way he parted with his money. She had often wondered just how much money her father had, and suspected his wealth was considerable.

'Where is it you're going?' she asked Paul again, lightly, screening her lack of trust. 'You did tell me, only I've forgotten.'

'Bordeaux.'

'And what's at Bordeaux?' He sighed deeply and glanced pointedly at his watch.

'Oh, of course I know what's there,' she added. 'Vineyards, fine wine and all that, but—'

He waved it aside impatiently, went into the hallway and grabbed his small suitcase, which he had packed himself the night before. As she followed him to the front door, he turned and looked her in the eye. 'We'll offer special culinary weeks there, with top chefs. My own company will put Bordeaux on the map.'

It almost crossed her mind to point out that Bordeaux was already well established but thought better of it.

'I know it's already a popular destination,' he sighed, almost as if he could hear the quibble in her mind. 'But it will be *the* place to go to this time next year. And now I must dash.'

He pecked her on the cheek, raised his suitcase handle, and wheeled it out into the third-floor hallway. She watched as he walked toward the small lift, and called out, 'Give me a ring when you get there. To let me know you've arrived safely.'

Without looking back, he pressed the lift button and replied, 'I can't promise. I'll be straight into a meeting.' Then, as the lift door opened, he laughed and said, 'You would soon hear about it if my plane crashed.'

After the lift door closed, she listened as it hummed and creaked towards the basement and underground car park. The hallway smelt of lavender polish, as if it had been recently cleaned, and again she pondered on the expense of the apartment block service charges, which she thought would be considerable. But she had no way of knowing. Paul made certain she was kept in total ignorance about the household finances.

4

After she returned to the living room she sat on the sofa and brooded, her hands like claws, tightly entwined. She felt tense, intuitively knowing there was something very wrong with her husband's lifestyle. After a while, she took a deep breath, unclasped her hands, and took stock of the situation. Not that there was any situation as such, she told herself; except for her own misgivings. When she analysed her relationship with Paul, she concluded that he was almost a total stranger. She knew nothing about him. His parents, his background. Nothing. He had just appeared one day, materialised out of the blue, and she fell for that smile of his, that naughty twinkle in his eye, and after a whirlwind romance of only four weeks, they were married.

Her eyes wandered, assessing her surroundings, something she hadn't done until recently. When she and Paul first viewed the flat, she hadn't seen its potential, how the rectangular living room with its dull magnolia walls might be transformed into this luxurious living space. It was a surprise he told her. After they returned from their Seychelles' honeymoon, and they entered the transformed flat, it took her breath away. As she crossed the beige Axminster carpet, and marvelled at the conversion, she seemed to sink two inches into the soft pile. The portico-style entrance to the dining area had been transformed, and an arch had been created with integrated shelving, which naturally boasted a discreet Bose sound system. It was as if a wand had been waved by a firm of interior designers, which was what Karen suspected to be the case.

As she sat, nervously biting her lip, she thought back to when she first began to question Paul's extravagant ways. Probably a few months ago. One evening, she heard him talking on his mobile in his study, his voice raised. Although his study door was closed, and his voice was muffled, she could have sworn he was being defensive, protesting about something. She thought she heard mention of money, and it started her thinking. A few days later she used her iPad to search the internet for the large L-shaped Italian leather sofa on which she now sat, and discovered it had cost a staggering six thousand pounds. Although she had been born and brought up in comfortable surroundings, never wanting for anything, she wasn't stupid. She surmised that his lifestyle was probably impossible to support from a single travel agent's outlet. Maybe he was a criminal of some sort? A drug dealer, perhaps; using his travel agency to smuggle narcotics. Her mind wandered along all kinds of dark streets as she fantasised about her husband's nefarious activities

She sighed and rubbed her chin, her frown deepening as she worried about a situation that was almost a fiction, something intangible she couldn't quite grasp. She checked her watch, and was surprised to see she had been sunk into the sofa for almost forty-five minutes after Paul's departure. His plane would be airborne in another hour. Heathrow was only a half hour's drive from Kingston, so he would already have parked the car and, as his small suitcase qualified as hand baggage, no doubt he'd be going through security by now.

Karen rose from the sofa, glanced at the view of Richmond Park from the window, and could just make out several deer in the dense undergrowth. She loved this view, and felt privileged to live in this wonderful location, with a good-looking man who had chosen the plainer of the twin sisters to be his lifelong mate. But still she felt insecure. What was happening to her, and what had brought about this sudden change?

Maybe it had nothing to do with Paul. Perhaps it was because of the distressing circumstances of her mother's condition and the inescapable acceptance of what lay ahead.

*

She looks so frail. Spidery fingers, paper-thin hands and brittle wrists. But not just her hands and wrists; every bone in her body looks brittle, weakened. Her form now a fragile shell, the cancer having destroyed any vitality enduring in flesh and blood. Her hollow cheeks a sure sign of death, and her eye sockets sunk deep into her skull, she bears no resemblance to the glamorous model who was once on the front cover of *Vogue*. But however physically weak her frame is, the eyes still contain a spark, a life force struggling to continue, and Karen knows what her mother craves. She'll have to lie to give her the contentment she needs. Peace at the end can only come from a reconciliation between her and her sister; she'll have to give a convincing performance and pretend not to hate Vanessa.

The look her mother gives her is probing, searching for any insincerity as she asks, 'Will you and Vanessa come to see me very soon? Together. Please, my darling. Before it's too late.'

Karen nods, giving herself time to think. 'I'll ring her tomorrow,' she says after a long pause. 'And we'll both come to see you – together. I promise.'

6

She expects her mother to smile at that. Instead, the look she gets is wary, with an almost imperceptible shake of the head. Her mother clears her throat, a small rasping sound, and eventually finds her voice.

'I want you to become friends again. Forgive her, please Karen. Not just for now. For the future. I want to know you'll be family again after I'm gone.'

The speech exhausts her mother, her eyes close briefly, then open again. And then she winces as agony dances in her tiny shrunken frame. Karen takes her cold hand, hardly daring to apply any pressure it seems so fragile, and squeezes gently. As she leans close to her mother, she is overwhelmed by the musty smell of decay.

'I'll go and fetch Jane, shall I?' she whispers.

Jane is the nurse who has been hired to look after her mother in her dying moments, and to administer morphine when required.

'Yes, get Jane. And have a word with your father about the three of us being together soon. *Very* soon.'

There is no doubt in Karen's mind about her mother's meaning, and she dreads having to make that phone call to her sister.

*

Karen turned away from the window towards the opposite wall, into which was sunk the large flat screen television. In the black of the screen she saw her slightly distorted image, like a misshapen figure from a fairground hall of mirrors, and it awakened in her memory a childhood fantasy of shape-shifting monsters and trolls, and knew it had something to do with her apprehensive mood.

Impetuously, she went into the dining area and confronted her reflection in the large square Porada mirror hanging on one of the walls, searching for something reassuring, something to restore her confidence. But all she saw was a face even more timid and passive than usual. When she was sixteen-years-old she remembered overhearing one of the girls at Roedean school describing her as marginally pretty but overwhelmingly mousy. That cruel description had shattered her, until seven years later, when she met Steve, who fell in love with her. Until Vanessa got her claws into him. And now, nothing she could blame Vanessa for, her world was falling apart again.

7

Now it was time to find out for certain about the enigma that was Paul. And there was one way, she was sure, she might get at the truth. If she was careful and left no traces of having tampered with his private papers.

In less than an hour he would be on his way to Bordeaux on an 11:45 flight. She knew this much was true because she had checked the flight times on the internet. But then he was a travel agent, so he would have the information at his fingertips.

She went into the kitchen, stood leaning on the island work surface and took a deep breath. Her breathing was tremulous, her nerves triggering doubts in her mind. She checked her watch again and saw it was 11:15, half an hour before Paul's take-off. But what if there was a flight delay? But hardly anyone decides to cancel because of a delay, not after having gone to the trouble of going through security. No, another half hour and she would do it. She smacked the work surface, psyching herself up to it.

First though, a quick cup of instant coffee. But after she made it, she winced at its bitter taste. Was this because of her mood? Or could it be because Paul always insisted on fresh coffee made in the state-of-the-art espresso machine, and now the taste of the instant was startlingly different? She poured the coffee down the sink, filled a glass with water and took a sip to wash away the bitter taste. She sat on one of the stools by the work surface, sipping the water slowly, and thought about the life of her mother slipping away. Despite the hot May sun streaming through the kitchen window, she shivered, but her eyes remained dry. Her resolve to learn more about her husband suddenly seemed just as important as her mother's decline.

There was no lock on Paul's study door; he had never had one fitted. He probably, she decided, trusted her enough not to disobey his ruling about tidying in there. And, of course, there was that time he freaked out, scared her into staying out of his study. Now she was curious to discover why he was so secretive. What was he hiding from her? Would she discover something latent about his past life, something of which he was deeply ashamed?

Her curiosity peaked as she pushed open his study door, carefully, like a scene from a film, half expecting a jump shot as Paul appeared from nowhere, grabbed her arm, and demanded to know what she thought she was doing.

Then, as she entered the small box room, she was surprised to see how tidy it was. She looked down at the carpet and saw it was dirt-free, as if it had recently been vacuumed and thought he must have done it on Sunday, two days ago, when she went to visit her mother.

The study was sterile and austere, and she thought this was quintessential Paul. It was barely big enough to be classed as a third bedroom, and even the estate agent who showed them the flat hadn't tried to sell it as a third bedroom. Most of the room was taken up by a gleaming work station in sandstone and slate, and a black leather swivel chair sat in front of it. Apart from a small, and very ordinary-looking, free-standing bookcase, with four shelves holding computer manuals, business motivational books and CDs, these two items of furniture seemed expensive and tasteful; but what intrigued Karen was the filing cabinet next to the desk. Sturdy plastic, bright blue, it stood about five feet high. It was so cheap-looking it jarred with his usual lavish frittering when it came to buying furniture or gadgets. She didn't remember seeing the filing cabinet that time he freaked out, or on the odd occasions she had knocked and entered to offer him coffee, and she wondered if perhaps it was a recent impulse buy from Ikea when the drawers in his desk became cluttered. The top of his desk was certainly free of clutter: A Toshiba laptop next to a printer/scanner and nothing else.

Karen shuffled forward uncertainly, wondering whether to look in the three desk drawers first or the filing cabinet. Knowing Paul's almost obsessional love of order, she had to be extremely careful to return any examined items to their exact location. She decided she would look in the top drawer of the desk first, raised the chrome handle and tugged. It slid open smoothly and she peered inside. Typically, one of the tidiest drawers she had ever seen: a rectangular lidless metal box containing a row of pens and pencils stood next to a stapler, hole puncher and two USB memory sticks. And that was it! Her husband had excelled himself in freedom from clutter.

Disappointed with what she found in the first drawer, she shut it and moved to the filing cabinet. She decided to pull open the second drawer down first, thinking the lower drawers might contain the more private or secretive stuff.

She smiled, knowing she was being over dramatic. Perhaps Paul had nothing to hide. Maybe it was just the fact that he enjoyed being fussy and obsessional, and wanted his 'sanctum' to remain sacrosanct.

Tugging open the filing cabinet drawer, she saw it contained a row of files hanging from metal rods. Carefully, she raised the first one in the row, placed it on top of the printer and opened it. She stared open-mouthed at the Barclaycard statement confronting her. The total owed was for almost ten thousand pounds. She knew he had at least six or seven credit cards, and if this amount was for only one of them….

Her eyes scanned the column of his recent spending, and to her horror she saw that there were five payments for extortionate amounts spent during one week at London clubs, totalling almost three thousand pounds squandered at Spearmint Rhino, China White, and some anonymously named companies which were probably clubs catering for customers who demanded discretion. But what was most unsettling about these payments were the dates. All of them during first week in April, and Karen was certain that was the week Paul claimed he was in Lanzarote setting up a deal. Whenever he went away on business, she usually made a note in her diary, which she kept in her handbag, so she could easily check to see if the dates tallied.

As she hurried through to the second bedroom, and her own workplace, where she had left her handbag, she began to feel nauseous and feverishly hot, clinging to the desperate hope that she might be mistaken about the date Paul was supposed to be in Lanzarote. But even if she was wrong, it still didn't explain why he spent all that money in West End clubs on his credit card. Three thousand pounds in one week on just the one credit card! She determined to look through his other files and statements, to find out just how much money he was spending and on what.

The quaking, nauseous feeling began to subside, giving way to anger now as she rummaged in her handbag and grabbed the rectangular pocket diary, clasping it tightly. She resisted opening it right away, returned to Paul's study and stood over the open file. She flicked through the diary pages to check the dates. And there it was: the first week in April she had written: 'Paul in Lanzarote this week. Back on Friday.'

So, he had lied to her, had been in London all that week. Now she had proof of her husband's deceit, his lies and ridiculous extravagances. As she glared at the Barclaycard statement, anger rose in her chest, her breathing became shallow, and she felt faint. She tried to breathe evenly, aware that she was hyperventilating. She stared at the statement, her eyes filled of tears. One of them dripped onto the page. She wiped her eyes with her sleeve, then used her index finger to wipe the statement. If it left a smear, might Paul suspect she had been through his files if he saw it? Not that it mattered now. As soon as he returned from Bordeaux she

10

would…What the hell was she thinking? The bastard was probably still in London. But why? What was his game? Running up crazy debts like he was hell-bent on self-destruction. The man was deranged. Just how much money did he owe? And then a voice screamed in her head: *Just how much money do* we *owe?*

Shaking now, she grabbed another file from the cabinet and opened it. Just then she was startled by the landline ringing in the living room and lost her grip on the file. It fell onto the carpet, and the papers inside scattered in all directions. For a moment, she worried about the consequences of not being able to place the papers in the right order, which would alert Paul to her violation of his hideaway, but then she obliterated the folly from her brain and went to answer the insistent ringing of the landline.

As she picked up the phone in the living room, she heard a jarring sound, the loud clearing of a throat.

'Hello?' she said, cautiously.

'Karen, it's your father here.'

Usually he referred to himself as 'Dad', and for a moment she wondered if it was bad news about her mother. It was expected at any time now, but it would still come as a shock.

'What is it?' she asked.

And then she heard, almost felt, the scorching anger scudding along the phone line.

'I'll tell you what it is. It's that fucking husband of yours. Where is he? He's not at his fucking travel agency. I've just been on to them, and that fat cow who works for him has no idea where he is.'

'Dad, what is it? What's wrong?'

'The fucking little wanker's business has gone belly-up. Can you remember he asked me to stand as guarantor for him last year? Well now my bank has called in the half a million I owe them, so where is that little fucker? And just wait till I get my hands on him.'

Two

Vanessa had never been close to her father, but now she had another good reason to hate him. She always suspected him of being a bully, and knew very little about his business empire, his financial speculations and property developments. He owned so much it was almost obscene, especially as there were so many poor people struggling to earn a crust. And now she despised him for his loathsome behaviour towards her mother, unable to contain his lust until after she was gone.

It was five in the evening, and although she didn't usually shut the sandwich bar until around six o' clock – depending on how many customers there were – as soon as she managed to get rid of the two teenagers who had spent at least forty-five minutes drinking one can of Pepsi Max each, she would close early and meet her friend Alice for wine and gossip. And she felt a desperate need to unburden herself.

She finished wiping the inside of the microwave clean, and glanced over at the teenagers, flirting and giggling. The boy, about 15-years-old, was quite good looking, with dark brown hair, styled trendily like a brush, which unfortunately gave him a comical appearance, and Vanessa wondered if this was what the girl found attractive. She may have been about the same age as her boyfriend, but seemed older and more mature, and looked stunningly attractive, exuding an easy confidence, knowing just how desirable she was.

Vanessa glanced at her watch, sighed and tried to restrain her frustration, praying no other customers crossed the threshold hoping to sit nursing a coffee for another half hour or more. Was this what she went to university for? Business studies for three years of her life, just so that she could run a failing sandwich bar just off Chiswick High Road. Every day the bills rose higher, and business rates for the district had almost doubled in April, but the income hadn't risen. If anything, it dwindled as custom decreased. Beyond her lunchtime trade, lasting for two hours at most, when she and her helper Jason were rushed off their feet, trade dropped off dramatically. There was so much competition in the district, and by late afternoon, as people drifted from work, they gravitated towards the trendier eating places, the wine bars and restaurants.

She was aware that her spending went beyond her income, and it seemed so unfair. She worked hard, got up at an ungodly hour to deal with the takeaway trade, the bacon rolls and sausage sandwiches for the early-morning workers, and still there was a huge deficit between her incomings and outgoings. There was the mortgage to find each month for her flat in the hinterland between Turnham Green and Kew, and debts on her credit cards increased beyond sanity. She was swimming in debt and in danger of drowning. Not that she was lavish, spending what she hadn't got on luxuries, she convinced herself. No, most of her credit card debts were from paying ordinary bills such as the utilities and household necessities. She had to live for God's sake! Had to have the odd evening's respite and a few glasses of wine. So, where had it all gone horribly wrong?

Once, perhaps less than a year ago, she might have considered approaching her father for financial help, but now it was out of the question. It was a matter of principle. She would rather suffer worse financial hardship than crawl to that bastard for help.

A squawk from the teenage girl, as she responded to something her friend said, fired Vanessa with an impatient desire to get rid of them. She had to get out and have that large glass of Pinot Grigio. She could almost taste it. She came from behind the counter and stood over the couple, hands on hips.

'If you don't mind, I'm about to close.'

The boy, clearly wanting to show off to his girlfriend, gave Vanessa a smile bordering on a sneer. 'I thought you shut at six. It's not five yet.'

Vanessa returned the smile, sickly sweet, and deliberately insincere. 'I'm shutting early tonight.'

'What? You mean you just chuck people out when you feel like it?' the boy protested. 'That's a bit of—'

His girlfriend shut him up by digging him in the ribs with her elbow. 'Come on. Let's go,' she said, stood up quickly and, without so much as a glance in Vanessa's direction, went out of the door.

The boy caught the open door as it was about to swing closed, turned back to Vanessa, gave her what he thought was a sexy smile, then looked her up and down, making it obvious he admired her slim legs and petite figure. 'See you again,' he said before exiting.

Vanessa turned the 'Open' sign to 'Closed' on the door, locked it, and sighed as she thought about the teenager. In a way, he reminded her of Steve: that boyish charm, with no shortage of chat-up lines, and a brash

13

confidence unmindful of limitations. She imagined the boy as a young man, with his wasted future of infidelity, constant lies and complications, just like hers and Steve's had been. A reckless relationship, causing irreparable damage. And would Karen ever forgive her? Hadn't her wretched sister ever heard of time being the healer, or did the bitterness run too deep?

*

As it wasn't yet five-thirty, and she couldn't see Alice anywhere in the pub, she went into the loo – mainly to kill time prior to meeting her friend, but also to check her appearance. She gazed into the mirror, fumbled in her handbag for her lipstick, then stretched across the wash basin closer to her reflection as she applied a thin patina of red to her lips. She leaned back and studied her image. Although she wore no other make-up, the lipstick gave her confidence, and now she felt equipped to handle the impenetrable obstructions in life.

When she returned to the bar, she still couldn't see any sign of Alice, so she decided she would order herself that well-deserved large glass of wine. She stood for a few minutes, waiting behind a row of men on stools hogging the bar, before she was served. She was about to swipe the payment on her latest credit card, when Alice arrived, breathless from hurrying along the busy street. Vanessa asked her friend what she was drinking.

Chuckling, Alice looked at the barman, nodded at Vanessa's large white wine, and said, 'I'll have what she's having!'

After they were served, Vanessa abandoned feelings of guilt for spending yet another fourteen pounds she hadn't got on plastic, and suggested to Alice they sit in the pub garden.

They found a free table, sipped their wine, and made preliminary small-talk. And then Alice frowned, and asked Vanessa if there was anything wrong.

Vanessa took a long time in answering. She had known Alice for just over a month (they had met in the waiting room of the doctor's surgery, got a fit of the giggles, and hit it off, arranging to meet socially a week later). During that time, as they got to know one another, Vanessa felt she could trust Alice implicitly. Besides, she felt a strong need to unburden herself, and expose her darkest thoughts, hoping for a cathartic kiss of life.

14

Alice smiled sympathetically, and Vanessa was confident their friendship would develop into a lasting one. Alice's expression was sincere and affectionate, and reminded Vanessa of a friendly Labrador. She was slightly overweight, and her face was rounded, but she was extremely pretty, and Vanessa guessed she would have no trouble attracting men.

'You don't have to tell me, if you don't want to,' Alice said. 'I just thought you might feel better if—'

'No, I need to tell someone. The only person in my family I could have told years ago was my twin sister. But we haven't spoken to each other for over five years, other than hellos and goodbyes, but very little in between.'

'I thought twins were supposed to be close. Inseparable.'

'They're monozygotic twins; twins from a single ovum. We are non-identical. In fact, you would be hard pressed to think we were related. We have nothing in common. She's the artistic one in our family.'

'And you're the successful business woman.'

'I think you can remove the word successful,' Vanessa said with an ironic chuckle. She could see Alice was about to ask her about the sandwich bar, and had no intention of being diverted from what was bothering her, so she added hastily, 'I think I could get on top of things like the sandwich bar, if it wasn't for my family.'

Alice knew she was being cued in and felt obliged to ask the right questions.

'So tell me about your sister. You say she's the artistic one. What does she do?'

'Graphic design. Mainly designs for band album covers, theatre posters, that sort of thing. To be honest, I know very little about what she's done in recent years.'

'So how did you fall out with her?'

'I had an affair with her fiancé and she's never forgiven me.'

Alice's mouth opened as she feigned astonishment, having guessed what was coming. 'Wow!' she exclaimed. 'Did she break up with him after that?'

'She found us in bed together. And would have nothing to do with him after that.'

'Understandably, I guess.'

For a moment, Vanessa sensed disapproval in her friend, felt the need to explain, and spoke hurriedly to dispense with the gossip about Karen and move on to what was really troubling her. 'Steve was a real charmer. I often wondered how they came to be lovers. But whatever's become of Steve, I always imagine he has a mistress as well as a wife now. He's that sort of bloke. He was very attractive, he came on to me so strongly, and I was only twenty-three at the time. Not that that's an excuse, I know.'

'But it takes two to tango, as they say. Shouldn't your sister have put most of the blame on to her fiancé?'

'I don't think she saw it like that. She saw it as a family betrayal. And if you want to hear about family betrayal it gets worse. This is the soap opera from hell.'

Vanessa saw the pupils in Alice's eyes dilate as her friend became intrigued and excited, although she kept her expression neutral, masking her relish of hearing a juicy tale

'My mother is dying of cancer,' Vanessa continued, her voice suddenly hoarse.

Alice gasped, placed her hand over Vanessa's and squeezed. 'I'm so sorry. How long…?'

'Perhaps only a few weeks. Or it could be any day now. Which is why Karen and I should be going over there every evening, spending as much time with Mum as possible, so that we are with her when she goes. But there are obstacles.'

'Your sister?'

Vanessa shook her head. 'Not just my sister. My father. I can't forgive him for his deceit. He can't wait for Mum to die, so his gold-digging bitch can move in with him. Bastard!'

*

What were the chances of her seeing them like that, in a city the size of London, with all the cinemas, theatres, concerts, pubs and restaurants to choose from? The odds are heavily stacked against that likelihood. Yet it happens. And it has happened to her! Fate guiding unsuspecting subjects to a predestined destination where life either changes for better or worse. Such is her destiny this fateful night as she sees them both entwined in each other's arms. At first she can't believe it. She thinks she must be mistaken. Her father with a woman half his age.

And what are they doing here in Greenwich?

This is a long way from either of their respective stomping grounds. Her family home, where her parents live, is on Richmond Green, and she lives between Kew and Chiswick, just the other side of the Thames and only a few miles from Richmond, so the chances of bumping into her father in Greenwich on a random night has got to be something to do with some sort of astral influence, a forecast of doom, like the foul predictions of the weird sisters in *Macbeth*.

She is on her way home after meeting an old friend from Sussex University for dinner and, as she makes her way towards the DLR station, she sees them coming out of the restaurant. They are on the other side of the street, about a hundred yards away, so at first she isn't a hundred per cent certain it's her father, but then – after kissing the young woman on the lips – he does that audacious jerk of the shoulders which he often does as he exits a building, a habit of his which she years ago analysed as his stepping out to confront the world with a renewed arrogance which he uses to battle his way through life. And there is no mistaking his longish black hair, which oddly carries not a hint of grey, even though he is fifty-nine.

The woman he is with has a figure most women would envy. She is blonde and looks like every man's dream chorus girl, with a skirt split on one side, revealing a tantalising and shapely leg. Even though they are a long way away, and disappear every so often as they make their way along the crowded street, she can still see that the young woman is beautiful and cannot be more than thirty-something.

And then she is even more certain it's her father, as she sees him light a cigarette, which is what he always does having sat in a restaurant for too long. But then don't hundreds of smokers do this as soon as they leave a public building?

Instinctively, she follows them on the opposite side of the street, wondering where they are heading now that they have clearly enjoyed a romantic, candle-lit dinner at that expensive-looking Italian restaurant where they undoubtedly flirted outrageously. And seeing the way the young woman raises her face toward her father, laughing and giggling at something he says, she guesses they are already lovers.

Sickened by the thoughts of her mother being betrayed by that foul monster who calls himself her father, she wants to run across the road and slap him, beat him with her fists. Revenge for the past. For when she was a child. And then pull the hair of that slut who flirts with him. Of course, when she was a teenager, she often thought her father, like many men, might have had bits on the side when he went away on business trips. But that was different. It was safe in her imagination, and she felt secure in never having to confront what was merely a vague suspicion, with nothing concrete to unbalance the orthodoxy of family life.

But this is different. She is disgusted by his duplicity, and thinks of her poor mother, bedridden and close to death, being looked after by a nurse, a total stranger, while her father fucks some money-grabbing whore. It must be his money she is after. Why else would a woman half his age open her legs to a man going on sixty?

The thought disgusts her, and tears cloud her sight. She wipes them away and decides she must follow them, although she has no idea how this evening will end. They are almost out of sight now and she knows she must hurry or she'll lose them. As she dashes across the road, a maroon Audi swerves to avoid her. Squeal of brakes, followed by an angry blast of a horn, and she almost runs into a cyclist hurtling towards her. She dodges breathlessly into a shop doorway, in case her father, alerted by the near accident, looks back and catches her following.

When she emerges from the doorway, she peers up the street, then, as she zigzags frantically to avoid the pedestrians walking towards her, and gets stuck behind couples ambling along, she can feel her anger swelling like bile in her throat. It's a Friday night and there are just too many people about. She stops and stares ahead, trying to make out her father's head above the crowds walking towards her. But she can't see him or that bitch anymore.

She has lost them.

Late that night, after drinking almost a bottle of white wine, she rings her parents' house. The phone rings for a long time before it is answered by Jane, who sounds sleepy.

'Who is it?'

'It's Vanessa. How's Mummy?'

'She's comfortable. She's lightly sedated and she's asleep. And I was just about to—'

Vanessa interrupts her. 'Can I speak to Dad?'

After having gone through agonies of hope and desperation, she prays that she may have been mistaken, persuading herself that it wasn't her father she saw in Greenwich after all. Just someone who looked very like him. And then Jane shatters the delusion.

18

'No, he's not here. He said he had some business to attend to and he won't be back tonight.'

Vanessa catches her breath, a moment of panic but also a feeling of triumph as she is being proved right. That *was* her father she saw with that slut. Definitely.

'Hello?' Jane says. 'You still there?'

'Yes. I'm sorry to have disturbed you, Jane. I'll pop over to see Mummy tomorrow – probably late afternoon after I've closed the shop.'

She hangs up and sits staring into space, her brain flooding with dirty and disgusting images of her father with that bitch. Her body trembles, an earthquake erupting, as she breaks down, heaving and choking with giant sobs.

*

An enticing whiff of nicotine drifted across from a table close to Vanessa, and she glanced at a red-haired young woman lighting a cigarette

'I sometimes wish I hadn't given up,' she said, wistfully.

Alice shook her head disapprovingly. 'Don't use these family problems as an excuse to start again. How long since you gave up?'

'Three years ago. I went out with a guy who didn't smoke. He said if we were to have a lasting relationship I had to give it up. I did, gave it up for him, and then after six months we split up.'

'And you didn't start again after the split?'

'No. Not because of him – deep down I knew it wouldn't last – but because I had always wanted to stop, and when Darren insisted we couldn't be a couple if I smoked, I used this as a motivation to finally kick the habit into touch. But now, with all this family stress, I could murder a fag.'

A blueberry aroma, sweetly tantalising, was borne on the slight evening breeze across the table between them and Alice inhaled deeply before it vanished.

'Why don't you smoke one of those vapour cigarettes?' she suggested. 'I believe they're harmless.'

Vanessa shrugged, and right away Alice knew the subject of smoking had ended, and guessed her friend wanted to disclose intimate details about her family. It crossed her mind that for the near future at least, this would be one-way traffic, with Vanessa talking about herself and her

19

problems, with barely a thought to spare for any troubles Alice might be experiencing. And then she pushed that thought to the back of her mind, telling herself she was being selfish to even think it. Her problems paled when compared to Vanessa's.

'What's your father like?' she asked. 'He's quite a successful businessman, isn't he?'

Vanessa nodded thoughtfully before answering. 'Too successful for his own good.'

'How d'you mean?'

'I think the word is ruthless. Of course, I'm only guessing but I think he may have done some dodgy deals in his time, and managed to avoid paying a lot of tax. And now the bastard's shitting on his own family.'

'And there's no possibility you could have been mistaken about seeing him with that girl in Greenwich.'

'None at all. I did have doubts at first, but that was me clutching at straws. Then, when I phoned and spoke to Mum's nurse that night, that was it! I knew it was him. How could he? With Mummy almost—' Vanessa avoided saying it; then an image of her father with that young woman, that slut in Greenwich, flashed into her head. 'I think I hate him now,' she hissed. 'I wish it was him who was dying instead of Mummy.'

'Have you always been closer to your mother?'

Vanessa nodded and took a sip of wine. 'I suppose I have. It's taken me all these years to realise that Mummy is his trophy wife. No, on second thoughts, I always knew that. It just went unspoken. You should see photos of her when she was a successful model.'

'Would I have heard of her?'

'Her heyday was in the seventies, before you were born. She was called Jaybee.'

Alice gasped excitedly. 'God! Yes, I *have* heard of her. But that can't have been her real name, can it?'

Her first name's Julia, and her second name's Barbara.'

'So, she used her first two initials as a *nom de plume*?' Alice guessed.

'Yes, and she was often in the papers, especially when Dad started going out with her. I think he enjoyed all the attention. Jaybee at such-and-such a club with millionaire Marcus Bradshaw.'

Vanessa gave Alice a questioning look to see if her father's name meant anything, but Alice shook her head and said, 'I remember seeing your mother's photographs though. She was gorgeous-looking.'

'Yes, she was stunning,' Vanessa agreed, and then an image of her father, his hand fondling the young tart's arse, flashed into her head, and she stared at Alice, her eyes blazing with suppressed anger. 'And now she's ill, the bastard has found a new model. It's no wonder I've come to hate him. Huh! You can take the boy out of the East End but—' She gave a dismissive wave of her hand. 'Well, you know the rest of the cliché.'

Alice looked genuinely surprised. 'Your father was an East Ender?'

'Not so as you would know. He's cultivated a well-spoken image, although you can just about detect a refined East End accent lurking in his speech. I never knew his parents; they died not long after Karen and I were born. His dad was a barrow boy, ran a fruit and veg stall, and his mother cleaned offices.'

'Does he try to keep it quiet?'

'No, far from it. He likes to boast about how he made it, despite the disadvantages. Although he's filthy rich, and he's helped us out a bit financially, he never went over the top in spoiling us. One of his favourite sayings is: "No pain, no gain".'

'Just how rich is your father? If you don't mind me asking.'

'I discussed this years ago with Karen – that's when we were still talking – and we estimated that he might be close to being a billionaire.'

Alice pursed her lips as if to whistle but made no sound.

'That was six years ago, so his fortune may have gone either way since then, although I don't think he's suffered any heavy financial losses,'

'And what about your sister? After you had an affair with her fiancé, did she find anyone else?'

'Not for a long time. It was like she'd gone into a convent. Then along came this…this…Paul.'

'You don't seem too sure of his name.'

Vanessa laughed. 'I had to think about it. I've only met him once. He's quite good looking, but I think in view of what happened with me and Steve, Karen keeps him away from me. I know nothing about my brother-in-law.'

Alice raised her eyebrows questioningly. 'So she and this Paul are married.'

'Six months ago.'

'Is that when you met him? At the wedding.'

'No. They got married abroad. None of the family attended. Which suited everyone really, except maybe for Mummy. I think Dad was OK

21

about it. Instead of coughing up for an expensive do, he gave them the deposit for a flat.' Vanessa frowned deeply and stared into her wine glass. 'You know it's very peculiar.'

'What is?'

'No one seems to know anything about this Paul. Mummy told me he just appeared one day, having met my sister near our house on Richmond Green.'

'Was this your parents' house?'

Vanessa nodded. 'Yes, you see, after Karen split up with Steve, she moved back home, and lived and worked from there. As a graphic designer, she's always worked from home rather than an office.'

There was a long pause as Alice assimilated this information. Then she said, 'So this Paul just appeared on Richmond Green one day. Bit odd that, isn't it?

Vanessa shrugged. 'I've only seen him the one time, and if you ask me, he's a bit weird.' She raised her wine glass and drained it.

'Another large one?' Alice offered.

'It would be impolite not to.'

While Alice went to get the drinks, Vanessa heard giggling and loud voices. She looked round and was instantly captivated by a family at the end of the pub garden. They seemed so contented, the four of them – a husband and wife with a grown-up son and daughter, or maybe not siblings but boyfriend and girlfriend. But, whatever the relationships, to Vanessa, the mood she was in, this family seemed like something that could only be captured in a thirty-second television commercial. Nothing dysfunctional like her own horrendous family. Except her mother, of course. And just as she thought about her mother, her mobile rang. She saw on the screen that it was Jane ringing and held her breath as she pressed answer.

'Jane! What is it?'

'I think you'd better come over right away.'

The nurse didn't sound distressed, but quite efficient and matter-of-fact. Vanessa guessed she was used to imparting this sort of information.

'Is she—' Vanessa asked, hardly daring to speak the word.

'I don't think she's got long to go now. You need to be here.'

I'll be over right away.' She hung up and dashed into the pub in time to stop Alice buying her a large glass of wine.

Although the family home, the house on Richmond Green, was impressive, a genuine late-Georgian mansion built in 1825, to Vanessa it represented not wealth or status but the comfort of childhood, when everything is orderly and established, until consistency disintegrates with the onset of maturity and responsibility. She remembered as a child often looking admiringly at the three floors and counting the fourteen windows, which almost became a ritual. The wrought iron balconies in front of the ground and second floor windows, her father added while she was at university, and because they were a purely ornamental add-on, she thought they were ostentatious.

She swung her Mini Cooper onto the small drive in front of the three-car garage, and saw in her rear view mirror a black cab stopping in the road. She waited while she watched her sister getting out. Karen glanced in her direction but gave not a jot of acknowledgement, before leaning into the taxi window to pay for the fare.

As Vanessa got out of her car, she looked up at the three-storey building, remembering the expansive playroom allotted to them both, their own special domain, chock full of every conceivable toy and book. It was their father's extravagance, indulging his children while they were still young and a novelty. She had loved the playroom, but also remembered how quickly she grew tired of it as she and her sister got older and drifted apart, often playing their own separate games in the same playroom. Poles apart. She often felt pangs of guilt about that. Perhaps it was her fault, the way she picked on Karen. Jealous of the way her sister's imagination turned the simplest games into creative fantasies.

As the taxi departed, the sisters moved tentatively towards one another. Vanessa, for a moment, wondered if the impending tragedy might bring her and her sister closer together. An embrace, a hug, maybe? But the occasion brought an even more unforgiving coldness to Karen's demeanour, and Vanessa knew there would be no reconciliation.

Karen's voice was a monotone when she spoke. 'I had a word with Mummy – made her a promise.'

Vanessa guessed what was coming and waited for Karen to continue.

'I promised her that we would make it up. She wants us to be friends and family again. I find that difficult – even now. But it's important for Mummy's sake.'

Vanessa wanted to slap and shake her sister, tell her she was the one continuing with this farcical conflict. *Get over it*! she wanted to scream. But the solemn occasion put constraints on her emotions, so that all she said was, 'What do you suggest?'

'I suggest,' Karen emphasised with a trace of irritation, 'that we give a convincing performance. Otherwise she'll be able to tell by the look in our eyes that we are lying. Do you think you can do that?'

'I know *I* can do it. What about *you*?'

Karen sniffed and said, 'For Mummy's sake I'll give an Oscar-winning performance. She'll never guess how much I despise you for what you did.'

'Oh, come on!' Vanessa protested. 'Steve wasn't worth it. He proved that. And now you've found someone else, so it's all water under the bridge.'

Karen stared at her sister, her expression deadpan. She was about to reply, tell her she could never truly trust her again, when the front door opened. It was Jane, with a solemn look set deep in her eyes. The sisters walked up the stone steps to meet her.

'I'm glad you both arrived together—' Jane began.

'You said we should come straight away,' Karen said. 'How is Mummy?'

'I'm so sorry. Your mother passed away fifteen minutes ago.'

'Oh, my God!' Karen moaned, throwing a glance at her sister. 'We didn't make it in time. She wanted us to be here at the end and we....' She began sobbing uncontrollably and Jane dutifully hugged her, wondering why her twin sister made no effort to console her.

But Vanessa was paralysed by the news and was dry-eyed, her face set hard. She had been expecting it, knowing it could happen at any time, and had previously rationalised that it was unlikely they might be with their mother at the very end, unless they kept a permanent vigil at her bedside.

She also felt excluded, unable to share the emotional outpouring of her sister. For days she had wept at home and felt drained of all emotion. She had sobbed uncontrollably like her sister, but privately. And now her senses were deadened by grief. *I'm all out of crying*, she thought, incongruously.

Karen sniffed and swallowed, raised her head from Jane's shoulder, and cried. 'Oh, shit! How cruel. I can't believe Mummy was on her own at the end. All this time she was lying in her bed, waiting, and we knew it was going to happen, so we should have been with her.'

Jane hugged her tightly. 'Your father was with her right at the end,' she said. 'Don't worry. She wasn't alone.'

'You're not just saying that?' Karen sniffed. 'Trying to make me feel better?'

'No, I can promise you. Your dad was with her.'

Catching Jane's eye, and knowing the nurse was trying to gauge her reaction, Vanessa turned her head away, staring into the distance over Richmond Green. She felt sickened by the hypocrisy of her father, who only a few nights ago she had seen in Greenwich with that slag.

She wondered if it was serious or a one-night stand. But what did that matter? It was his total disloyalty and disregard for her mother's terrible condition that hurt.

Across the Green, a group of five young children played football, and an elderly man walking his Staffordshire Bull Terrier stopped to watch them. Vanessa's memory drifted to a time when she and Karen were only five- or six-years-old and she remembered it was always their mother who played with them, never their father. Oh, yes, he liked to show them off. "These are my two lovely little twins." But she couldn't recall a time when he so much as stooped to their level to play a game. It was always their mother. Without fail. Making up for his lack of family involvement.

She blinked and turned towards her sister and Jane. She was aware Jane had said something, but had missed it. 'Sorry? What did you say?'

The nurse misinterpreted Vanessa's detachment as shock, and lowered her voice. 'I asked if you would like to visit your mother's room, so that you can see her for the last time.'

'I don't know. I suppose so. I mean, yes – yes, I do.'

Jane nodded, pleased she was getting the right response. 'It will help you both,' she said. 'Paying your respects, even though she may be departed.'

They went indoors and Jane closed the door carefully, so as not to disturb the hallowed atmosphere of death in the house. As they followed her upstairs, Karen asked, 'Where's Dad now?'

'In the living room. He said he needed a stiff drink. The last half hour he spent with your mother has been a difficult time for him.'

She opened the door of their mother's room and stood aside for them to enter. They shuffled over to the bed and looked down, horrified to see the corpse was nothing like their mother. An empty shell, shrunken and

25

shrivelled beyond recognition, the cadaver bore no resemblance to the mother they loved. A skeleton hand lay outside the bedclothes and Karen tentatively moved her fingers towards it, softly touching, hardly daring to do more. She took her hand away and Vanessa caught Jane looking at her, as though she too was expected to touch her mother's hand.

'I would sooner remember Mummy as she was,' Vanessa said.

'That's perfectly natural,' Jane replied.

Karen turned away from the bed. 'Shall we go and find Dad?' She stopped at the door and looked back. 'Goodbye, Mummy.'

'Yes, goodbye, Mummy,' Vanessa mumbled indistinctly.

When they went into the living room, they found their father talking on his mobile, a glass of brandy in his other hand. 'Yes, that's right: two first class tickets St Pancras to Paris,' he said. 'If you can sort it I'd be grateful. Things are hectic right now. Depart June 7th. Return Wednesday June the 14th.' He glanced at his daughters. 'I've got to go. I'll call you later.'

Talking to his fucking tart, Vanessa thought, *before Mummy's even cold.*

Avoiding eye contact with her father, she looked up at the picture over the marble mantelpiece. An original Jack Vettriano of a woman leaning against a railing on a pier, a man lighting her cigarette, clearly a pre-coital one. She had never liked the painting, but now she hated it, seeing it as typical of her father's flashy other lifestyle.

Eyes moist, their father put his mobile and brandy glass on the coffee table and opened his arms wide to embrace Karen. 'Oh, it's terrible,' he moaned. 'Terrible.' He squeezed her tight, then stepped back and looked at her. 'I know: it still comes as a shock even though it's expected. Your mother was a beautiful, wonderful woman. Wonderful. I'm going to miss her.'

Vanessa stiffened. What a phoney her father was. All that dripping sincerity and tearful delivery. She felt nauseated by the performance. And now it was her turn to be embraced. It was all she could do to allow it, and stood with her arms stiffly at her sides, not responding in any way.

After the embrace, he moved back and, head cocked on one side, locked eyes with her. 'You all right, Nessa?'

'I could do with a drink.'

'Help yourself.'

As she poured herself a gin and tonic at the drinks cabinet, she asked, 'Have you telephoned Aunty Christine?'

'Give us a chance.'

'Mummy and her sister are very close.'

'I know, I know. I'll do it in a minute.'

'So who were you on the phone to when we came in just now?'

'A client. Booking us Eurostar for a business meeting.'

Karen coughed to clear her throat, stared at her father, her eyes suddenly hard, and her voice was brittle when she said, 'I would have thought Aunty Christine was a priority, not a business call when Mummy's been gone for only half an hour.'

One of their father's philosophies was attack being the best form of defence.

'So what would you know about business? You or that little shit you're married to. His fucking business has gone down the Swanee, owing me half a fucking million. I've never trusted the little turd, and I shall crucify him when I find out what he's about.'

Karen's voice shrivelled as she was reminded of her husband's fraudulent
behaviour. 'I'm sure he's not – I mean, there must be some....'

'Mistake? I don't think so,' her father said, picked up his brandy glass and knocked back what was left. 'We know fuck all about that arsehole. I've never trusted the little prick. I want to know what he's up to. And I intend finding out.'

Three

After six months, I'd had enough, and I vowed my wife would have to meet with an accident.

I just had to wait for the right opportunity. No sense in rushing things. That's the way you get caught. But I was fast running out of patience.

When my PR company in Aberdeen hit a bad spot, Jenny became unbearable. Moaning about her precious savings that she used to fund my business whenever it needed a cash injection. I told her all businesses go through a bad patch, but she couldn't, or wouldn't, see it like that. I told her to give it time, allow the business to establish itself. Then we had a great row about my bad time keeping and she accused me of being late for important meetings. I explained to her for the umpteenth time how the director of a company must delegate, otherwise what is the point of being the person in charge. You must always show them who is boss and create a distance, a certain mystique about yourself, otherwise they'll take advantage and think you're not a person to be reckoned with.

But she could never understand that. Always whining about her paltry savings.

Although I suspected they were far from paltry, and guessed, from something she let slip in the early days when we first went out together, that those savings were substantial, running into a five-figure sum. Maybe not enough for a lifetime of luxury, but an adequate sum with which to speculate in an ongoing concern like my PR company.

The times I tried to persuade her we should have joint bank accounts, but she wouldn't hear of it, like she didn't trust me. I was always open with her, and I couldn't comprehend this lack of trust. I was her husband for Christ's sake! And it wasn't as if she worked to earn that money. It was an inheritance from her father, who died from a heart attack about six months after his wife's demise. Pathetic. Probably couldn't live without his beloved. No doubt he felt at a loss when she was gone, both having lived out of each other's pockets for a lifetime. When Jenny described them to me, I could picture them walking along the sea front at Cruden Bay, hand in hand. I've seen elderly couples like that, inseparable, tied together with an invisible umbilical cord. Enough to make you puke.

And I'll bet it was her mother who wore the trousers. Just like my mother. The way she used to speak to my father sometimes made me cringe. But it's funny, I used to hate him more than her. I despised him because he didn't stick up for himself. A pathetic little civil servant who was probably bullied at work. Used to come home depressed, probably hoping for sympathy. Fat chance. My mother lost patience with him. And I used to play up to her. Gave her the benefit of my smile. I remember reading in a business motivational manual how a smile is one of your greatest assets and costs you nothing. Very true.

It was how I wooed Jenny. I scanned the local papers, always the obituary columns and notices of funerals, on the lookout for a wealthy widow. Better still, I found Jenny, weeping buckets at her father's funeral. An only child, just like me. And no one to look after her. Her father was a widower, her mother having died a few years back. Things couldn't have looked more promising for yours truly. Time to make an entrance.

The funeral was in a small church near Cruden Bay, which is roughly twenty miles north of Aberdeen – where I lived at the time, having come north to escape my parents, wanting to put as much distance between me and them as possible, and I thought Aberdeen would do the trick. I was self-aware enough to understand my motives, psychological I suppose, creating a vast distance between that semi in Hitchin and somewhere new, somewhere to sniff out the golden opportunities. I had been thirsty for long enough. Now it was time to drink my fill.

I drove over to Cruden Bay on the day of the funeral but didn't venture inside the church. I watched from a safe distance, assessing the situation. The funeral didn't seem that well attended and I suspected (rightly as it turned out) that Mr and Mrs Henderson had been an insular couple who would hopefully have stamped this hallmark onto their little treasure. And that characteristic, I figured, would make her ripe for what I had in mind. Providing there were no siblings of course. But when I followed them from the church, I couldn't see anyone who looked like a brother or sister, so things started to look promising.

Even more promising, from a distance the bereaved daughter looked presentable, although I didn't like her long black hair cut into an annoying fringe worn too low over her eyes. Her rounded face was smooth and she had full, letter-M-shaped lips that looked as if she had once sucked her thumb. She had firm rounded breasts, good strong legs, and looked like someone used to robust outdoor exercise. She would do.

29

I had to be very careful when I tailed them though, because the house they lived in was half a mile outside Cruden Bay, in a remote area up a narrow road, with no sea view, just a rugged outcrop to look at, dreary and depressing. Even the sheep looked suicidal. And the Hendersons' insularity could probably be explained by not only the geography but the house itself; a gloomy, granite monstrosity, three-storeys high, one of those looming edifices you see in that part of the world. When I first arrived in Aberdeen, I stayed in a similar bed and breakfast mausoleum and felt like opening a vein. Thank Christ it was only for three weeks; any longer and I'd have been carted off in a straightjacket.

So, although I didn't particularly like the Hendersons' tomb-like residence, I thought at the time that beggars can't be choosers, and my long-term plan was to get a husband's fifty per cent slice of that house, and see how I could advance my career in the world of public relations, which I soon discovered was fine if you know how to bullshit.

I had a staff of two, and an office near Castlegate, about as central as you can get in Aberdeen. We had four clients, which just about covered the staff wages and the rent, but I still needed to expand if I wanted to savour some of the luxuries in life which, let's face it, we all desire. Although most of our potential business was based in Aberdeen, and I could quite easily have coped with walking to meetings, or taking an occasional taxi, I still needed an impressive set of wheels, so my company leased a car – a brand new, top of the range Saab.

Not long after Henderson's funeral, on every weekend – and a few weekdays when things were quiet at the office – I drove over to Cruden Bay, hoping to bump into Jenny. She drove a modest little Renault Clio, and one Saturday I waited yet again on the main road for her to drive out of that narrow road to nowhere. I had followed her a few times when she went shopping, but never found an opportunity to engage her in conversation, as there were too many people around, and I needed her to be alone. But on that Saturday, my patience paid off, because instead of driving to the shops, she drove to the sea front, parked the car, and set off for a walk along the beach. It was the opportunity I'd been waiting for.

Jenny, I discovered, was thirty-five, ten years older than me. I also discovered how comparatively easy seduction is. The right moment is everything, so that Jenny, suffering the recent bereavement, saw my entry into her life as a sort of spiritual transformation. How had I, with my winning smile, my charm and sympathetic listening skills, suddenly

30

materialised like a gift? It never occurred to her that I had singled her out, planned everything in advance. And the silly cow thought it was destiny. Kismet. How gullible she was. Crying out to be conned.

Within two months we were married. At first, I made myself indispensable to her. She had only ever had the one boyfriend, with whom she shared his passion for rock climbing and abseiling. He asked her to go to New Zealand with him, to start a new life, but she wouldn't leave her parents. The ex-boyfriend sounded like a rustic arsehole, another boring outdoor type, and, as far as their sex life went – I guessed from some of the things she let slip – he was a wham-bang-thank-you-ma'am between the sheets. And she confessed during an unguarded moment – in other words *in vino veritas* – she had never experienced an orgasm. Although she claimed she didn't mind. It was a classic case of what you've never known, you can never truly miss! And she said the sex hadn't mattered. What mattered was that she loved him, until the country bumpkin decided to seek pastures new.

Knowing this, I resolved to make her dependent on me in every way, especially in bed, making certain I gave her the sexual gratification she had never known by going down on her. She had never experienced that form of tongue pleasure before and for many months she was totally in my power. The way she moaned and clutched the sheets as she reached a climax gave me a feeling, not of pleasure, but of owning someone. Controlling them. And I always took my pleasure after the cunnilingus by getting her to masturbate me so that I ejaculated over her stomach. I rarely penetrated her – if I did, I always made certain I wore a condom. What I hated and feared more than anything else was in becoming a father. I loathed and detested the thought of bringing any little bastards into the world, and swore that if ever I did, I would smother them at birth.

For the first three months of marriage I manipulated her, moulded her to my way of acquiring the life-worth-while luxuries and possessions I've always coveted. And as she was the only beneficiary of her father's will, within six weeks the deeds of the house were transferred to her name, and she received a thirty-eight-thousand-pound legacy. Which wouldn't last forever, but it would help bail my company out of difficulties, seeing as I had recently lost a couple of clients who took their business elsewhere. I didn't tell *her* that, of course. I told her I needed money to expand the business, and it was just a question of borrowing money from her savings. I managed to convince her that there was no sense in taking out bank loans and paying high rates of interest. At first she was compliant, but then one day in late October, after we were married for almost six months, I arrived back home in a year-old Range Rover which I bought, and she asked me what had happened to the Saab. I explained it was a company car, and the Range Rover was mine. She went ballistic at that, wanting to know how I could afford it. Despite my explanation of needing a reliable four-by-four for the winter when we could be snowed-under, she threatened me, telling me she was withholding the five thousand she had reluctantly agreed to loan my company. I could see she expected me to retaliate by losing my temper, shouting and swearing. But that was never my style. Better to keep things close to one's chest and make plans. Things had reached boiling point and I knew it was time to act, because her nagging about money was getting on my tits. I had to find an ingenious but simple method of killing her, so that it looked like an accident.

And then, suddenly, I found the opportunity I needed. Who'd have thought something as banal as a blocked gutter could resolve my situation. It was early November, and after heavy winds and swirling autumn leaves, followed by a fortnight of drenching rain, our guttering needed attention, as the rainwater, instead of running down the drainpipes, streamed over the gutter where it was blocked and ran noisily past our bedroom window and the living room.

'Something has to be done about it, as soon as possible, before it gets any worse,' Jenny said, which sounded like the way my mother spoke to my father.

But I kept my temper in check and agreed with her, while my brain spun a quick web of brilliant deception, and a great scheme presented itself to me like all my birthdays had come at once. I told her I was shit-scared of heights. Hated even going up a small step ladder, and the guttering must have been at least thirty feet high or more. I knew, of course, she went rock climbing and abseiling, and she offered, providing I held the ladder steady, to sort out the guttering. This was on a Monday night, and I suggested, because it was still raining, and I had to go to the office in Aberdeen every weekday, that the following Saturday would be the best time to tackle the guttering, and it might have stopped raining by then.

During the next four days, on my way home from Aberdeen, I stopped at a small pub on the outskirts of Cruden Bay – I think it was called The Fairway. While I was there on the Tuesday, I pretended to ring Jenny on my mobile, having an imaginary conversation with her about not attempting to deal with the guttering on her own and to wait until Saturday. I knew some of the locals in the pub were listening to the conversation, and would no doubt talk about me after I'd left the premises, gossiping about some henpecked bloke pleading with his wife not to do anything silly because her spineless husband couldn't climb a ladder.

I didn't think this was strictly necessary, it was a precaution. If the local plod made enquiries after the accident, this would add validity to my concerns about Jenny, and the tragedy which happened because she foolishly ignored my pleas not to do anything silly, even though she was an experienced rock climber.

I also took the precaution of phoning Jenny as soon as I left the pub, to ask if there was anything she wanted me to pick up from the shops on my way home. That way the call on her mobile would be registered at roughly the same time as the locals in the pub overheard my fake call.

Saturday. I pretended to sleep late, and I told Jenny I was feeling unwell, and could she wait until the afternoon to deal with the guttering. Jenny asked me what was wrong, and I made an excuse, said I had a sore throat, and was probably coming down with a cold. I then did everything at snail's pace, as if it was an effort to move. For the plan to work, I needed Jenny to go up that ladder once the pubs had been open for at least a few hours.

I took a couple of aspirin, ate a bowl of porridge slowly, and spent a long time in the bathroom. Then, after I was dressed, I said I needed to do some work in my study, essential stuff to pitch to a client on the Monday, and I promised Jenny we would deal with the guttering immediately after an early lunch.

As I heard her rummaging about, tidying our bedroom, and cleaning the bathroom, I thought about the next few weeks. I knew she had an uncle and a few cousins, but none of them were close. Her parents had kept so much to themselves, I doubted any of their relations would stay long at the funeral. Perhaps there'd be two paragraphs in the local rag about the tragedy. And then the local gossip. That poor young man, a widower after only six months of blissful marriage, too devastated and lonely to remain in our windswept town, sold the house and moved. And soon the gossip would dry up. It wasn't that interesting. Just an accident. Someone falling off a ladder. Soon the Hendersons would be forgotten, and I would be – well, not exactly rich – but at least solvent for a while.

A plan that was almost perfect in its simplicity. And in a way, it was weird; taking a step into the unknown. And I don't mind admitting it gave me a buzz. The nerve ends in my fingers tingled and all my senses became sharp. It was like the scent of a flower on a summer's day.

I heard Jenny vacuuming downstairs, looked at my watch and saw that it was gone 12.30. Time for lunch.

I could see she was keen to get on with clearing the guttering, and asked if beans on toast was enough for lunch. I told her it was all I could manage seeing as I was still feeling under the weather. We had a quick cup of tea after that, and then she said it was time to get the extending ladder out of the garage. First, I told her, I needed to get a pair of gloves to wear, and she demanded to know why. I said I was afraid to get splinters from the wooden ladder as I held it steady, and she laughed and accused me of being a wimp. Making out it was a joke, but at the same time an underlying disdain.

We'll soon see who's a wimp, I thought.

We took an end each of the ladder and I backed out of the garage with it. It was quite heavy and I wondered if she could struggle with it on her own. I decided it was just possible if she raised one end and dragged it along the ground. I didn't want my prints on the ladder, just in case the police didn't believe the story of her tackling the gutter on her own.

We raised the ladder against the building and then we both pushed the extension up as high as it would go, and it just about reached under the gutter. It looked far from safe, which was perfect for the accident waiting to happen. And there wouldn't be long to wait now.

Jenny stared at me, one foot on the bottom rung of the ladder, and for a moment I thought I saw suspicion in her eyes. But I was mistaken. What she said was, 'You should have worn old clothes, you idiot. You're going to get covered in shit when I clear the gutter out.'

But I could hardly go to the pub dressed like a tramp, although some of the regulars looked unkempt.

'I'll be OK,' I shrugged.

'Well,' she said, starting up the ladder, 'on your own head be it.'

I laughed. 'Literally,' I said.

When she was halfway up, I noticed the way the ladder bowed. It certainly looked precarious, and even if I hadn't lied about fear of heights, climbing that ladder is not something I would have felt comfortable with. She reached the top and peered into the gutter. I waited for her to grab a handful of sludge, her hands not holding on to the ladder. She looked down, balanced precariously without holding on, and was about to drop the sludge when I positioned myself between the wall and the ladder and pushed with all my strength. I heard her shouting, screaming, and I pushed harder and sideways. I looked up and saw she had lost her balance, tried to grab hold of the gutter, and then one of her feet slipped off a rung, and instead of grabbing the gutter, she grabbed the top of the ladder, and her weight pulled it forcefully away from the wall. The ladder swung away from the wall, and she hurtled towards the concrete path leading up to the house. Her head smashed with a sickening crack on to the concrete, and the ladder came crashing down on top of her.

There was no way she could have survived that fall. And even if by some miracle she did, there was no one to call for help or phone for an ambulance because I was off to that pub and wouldn't return for a long while. By then she would be well and truly dead.

Stupid woman! Fancy going up that ladder all on her own. She should have waited for her husband to get home.

Four

Sunk into the middle of the enormous sofa, Karen appeared small and vulnerable. Her eyes were red, but she had stopped crying hours ago. Her lips were stretched tight, the only indication of how tense she felt, though she inwardly squirmed, dreading the confrontation with Paul, who had phoned to say he was on his way home from the airport. She hated scenes and would go out of her way to avoid heated arguments, choosing instead to ignore anyone who slighted her, which was how she dealt with her sister. But now she was determined to challenge Paul about the lies and deception, and stared with glassy eyes at the coffee table strewn with his invoices and statements. She knew he'd go berserk, probably react as he had when she went to clean his room that time, but she was determined to deal with it.

Click! She blew out a nervous breath and tensed as she heard the front door key in the latch. Click! The door opened and closed. Then she heard him whistling brightly for a few moments as he walked along the hall, dragging his suitcase behind him. 'I'm home,' he called out before entering the living room.

She remained still and silent, preparing herself for the eruption. As soon as he spotted the evidence laid out on the table, first would come the surprise, then the realisation that she knew. She wanted to enjoy that initial moment, seeing him caught in the net. Trapped. She was frozen with dread, but in her mind, she saw herself pointing an accusing finger at the evidence and wished she was unhampered by her ridiculous self-consciousness.

Leaving his suitcase in the hall, he came into the room, and was about to say something when his eyes alighted on the invoices and statements.

She was disappointed. There was no expression of surprise to relish, just a calculating look in his eyes as he weighed up his options or excuses. She could see the wheels turning in his head, the cogs slotting into place as he worked out his next counterfeit move.

'What the fuck is all that?' he said. Voice raised indignantly, she noticed, but controlled. 'That's my private correspondence.'

'Not any more it isn't. I want some answers.'

'Answers?'

'Yes, about that fake trip to Lanzarote in April.' She watched for his reaction, but his face was inscrutable.

'You must have got the dates wrong,' he said.

'Don't treat me like an idiot, Paul,' she shouted, surprising herself by her vehemence. 'I checked it in my diary, so don't try and lie your way out of it. The week you were supposed to be in Lanzarote, you were clubbing it in London.' She pointed to the pile of paperwork on the coffee table. 'There's the proof. Who is she?'

He looked genuinely confused. 'She?'

'Have you got another woman?'

'Of course not.'

'There's no of course about it. If you can tell lies about—'

'You wouldn't understand,' he broke in.

'Try me. Try telling the truth for once.'

He sighed deeply, displaying frustration for her benefit. 'If you must know, I've been channelling all my energies into what I really want to do in life. These club visits were to do with networking, building up relationships and doing deals.'

'And I'm guessing,' she said, her voice a cold monotone, 'that you haven't been to Bordeaux either. I can check up on that, you know.'

'OK – look! I knew you wouldn't understand, which is why I had to be a little economical with the truth.' He saw she was about to object and continued hurriedly. 'I've been working towards the big opportunity. The biggest in my life. Our lives. This is a chance to make shed loads of money if it comes off.' He saw her sneering expression of doubt and corrected himself hastily. 'Not *if* it comes off. I mean *when* it comes off. It's just a question of sitting tight. It will happen eventually. Maybe soon.'

As he remained standing in what he thought was the controlling position, because his wife was sunk so low on the sofa, he realised the roles were reversed, and she was the more dominant, especially as he was having to explain himself like a child standing before a head teacher.

'I think I need a drink,' he said, and went to the in-built unit that housed the alcohol and poured himself a glass of single malt.

'And what is this wonderful, money-making scheme?' Karen said, her voice dripping with sarcasm.

'I'm trying to set up a movie.' Eyes-piercing, Karen stared at her husband with a mixture of pity and disbelief. 'As a producer,' he continued. 'You know I told you I went to film school when I was nineteen—'

Her patience about to crack, Karen cut in, 'I know, and you made a short film which won a competition. Which is all you ever mentioned about your past life.'

'That's because it meant so much to me.'

'So what? Making one short film. That doesn't mean you can make it big in Hollywood.'

'Who said anything about Hollywood? I'm talking about a British gangster movie with a modest budget of three million.'

'And what about the half a million you owe my father?' she yelled.

'Half a million! What are you on about?'

'Your travel agency has gone bust,' she screamed, leaning forward across the coffee table and sweeping the bank statements to the floor. 'And Dad's bank has called in the half million. He's fucking livid and says you owe him that money.'

'Shit! When did this happen?'

'I can't believe I'm hearing this. Three days ago, that's when it happened, while you were out clubbing. The day before Mummy died. Yes, Mummy's gone now.'

He put on a contrite face, but the insincerity was transparent. 'Oh, God! I know it was bound to happen, sweetheart, but I'm so sorry to hear it.'

'No, you're not. You couldn't give a shit about anyone but yourself. You weren't even here to support me when she passed away.'

'I'm sorry, but it couldn't be helped. When's the funeral? At least I'll be here for that.'

'Next week. Not that you could give a fuck.'

'That's not true, Karen, I—'

She staggered to her feet and screamed at him, 'You just don't get it, do you? We are now flat broke, our mortgage is in arrears, and Dad's pissed off about the half million.'

'OK! Calm down! Your father can afford it. Let's face it, it's not like half a mill's the end of the world. That can't be more than half a per cent of his total worth.'

Stunned by what he said, her bottom lip quivered, and she sat back down. Her shoulders shook as tears clouded her eyes, then she covered her face with her hands as she sobbed.

Paul watched her dispassionately, then asked, 'Can I pour you a drink?'

38

Knowing how the worst character traits surface in a family when a relative dies, and there then comes a mad scramble to get hold of the possessions of the deceased, like carrion crows picking the bones of a rotting corpse, Vanessa realised she was doing just that as she set off for Richmond late on Thursday afternoon. But she wanted to take possession of the Edwardian necklace belonging to her mother before Karen got hold of it. The necklace, a beautiful pendant set with aquamarines and seed pearls, belonged to their maternal grandmother, who died when the sisters had just turned twenty. The necklace had been left to their mother, and Vanessa wanted it for sentimental reasons because she had loved her grandmother very much. But then, so had Karen.

As she drove over Kew Bridge, Vanessa reflected on what she was doing, and how wrong it was to grab the necklace before her sister got a look in. Then, as she thought about Karen's hostility, lasting for a hateful five years, she decided it was penance enough to justify commandeering the necklace.

She prayed her father was out chasing business, buying up land or properties, and whatever else he did to make money. He was usually out all week, but never on a Friday, a routine he had taken with him from when he worked in the City. Getting everything resolved before the following week, all the trade deals, the plans, the balance sheets – it was always on a Friday. Sometimes quite late into the night, so that the hard work justified playing hard during the weekend. Not that she and Karen had ever benefited from his leisure time at the weekends. Leisure to their father meant hours spent on the golf course, or hobnobbing at celebrity functions or a few drug-fuelled parties and rock concerts. Occasionally, as a family they might be taken to the cinema or theatre, but their father thought that he deserved to spend most of his spare moments following mainly adult pursuits because of his hard work.

As she drove along the road past the great brick wall of Kew Gardens on her right, she checked the time. It was just gone four. It was lucky she managed to persuade Jason to stay on for the afternoon session, and she could be back in time to close the sandwich bar for the evening. And in her possession would be her grandmother's necklace, which she would show to Alice in the pub, anticipating her friend's cooing cries of delight as she examined its extravagant beauty.

She still had a key to the parental home, so she could let herself in, which was not a problem. The main obstacle would be if her father was home for some reason. Not because he might object to her taking this one precious item, because her mother's jewellery box contained numerous valuable pieces; but because she loathed him for his infidelity, and she couldn't look at him now without wanting to scream and slap his face.

She arrived on Richmond Green only twenty minutes after crossing Kew Bridge. She drove past Richmond Theatre and The Cricketers pub, then turned right towards her parents' home. When she was only about ten yards from the entrance, she slammed on the brakes as she saw a small Fiat pull out from in front of the garage and into the road. Vanessa's Mini stalled as her foot missed the clutch, and she pounded the steering wheel angrily, as she glimpsed the face of the Fiat's driver.

It was her! The slag she saw with her father in Greenwich. Her father couldn't even wait until after the funeral to shag his bimbo. And in their family home. Maybe in her mother's bed.

And to add to the injury, Vanessa knew that collecting the necklace was out of the question now. Her father has just given her another reason to hate him.

Five

Waiting at the arrivals barrier, Vanessa made eye contact with her aunt as she exited through customs clearance, gave her a small wave and a smile, then hurried forward through the crowds to greet her. They embraced and Vanessa felt the tension in her aunt's body, a lack of response, and sensed her aunt was deliberately suppressing her affection, just as she herself had done with her father's embrace the day her mother died. But then she was probably reading too much into it. After all, a late-night departure from New York, arriving at 2.p.m. our time, it was no wonder her aunt felt shattered and tense. Coupled with the fact that she was visiting to attend her older sister's funeral. No, Vanessa would have to make allowances for her Aunty Christine's unfamiliar reserve.

She glanced down and nodded at the small suitcase her aunt wheeled behind her. 'Hand luggage? You're not staying long then?'

'Just for the funeral tomorrow. Then I leave early the next day.'

'I wish you could stay longer.'

Her aunt pursed her lips, avoided Vanessa's eye, and said, 'So do I, but…where are you parked?'

Vanessa pointed towards the tunnel leading to the travellator. 'Short stay car park.'

'And Karen still can't drive?'

Vanessa shrugged, knowing it was her aunt's trick question to see if they were on speaking terms.

'I don't think she's interested in learning.'

As they stood on the travellator, heading for the short stay car park, Vanessa glanced surreptitiously at her aunt, who stared into the distance. Five years younger than her sister, Christine resembled her in so many ways. They were both natural blondes, with bright blue eyes, but Christine had a slightly rounder, fuller figure, and was only five foot six, whereas Vanessa's mother was five-ten.

'*Was*,' Vanessa thought, and shivered as she pictured her mother's corpse inside the coffin. Tall and elegant, even in death.

As they fetched Vanessa's Mini, then drove out of the airport, the conversation was desultory, like two polite strangers straining to find something to say. But as soon as they were cruising along the M4, as if the straightness of the road in some way soothed her aunt's emotional state, Vanessa heard her exhale loudly, easing the strained atmosphere and getting rid of the awkwardness of bereavement.

'Even when we were kids, your mum and I, we were ever so close you know. There was never any jealousy or hatred. We loved each other. And even though I've lived in New York for the past sixteen years, we were just as close. That's how sisters should be.'

Vanessa guessed where the conversation was heading, and dreaded the recriminations about the rift between her and Karen.

'I only hope,' her aunt went on, 'that my sister's passing away has brought you and Karen together. It's what Julia wanted. More than anything she wanted you to come together and be friends once more.'

'I tried to make that happen. I know it was all my fault, but you would think that after five years Karen might forgive and forget. Especially now she's found someone else and got married.'

'Paul, isn't it? What's he like?'

'I don't really know. I found him a bit weird. But I only met him once. It's as if Karen, because of what happened with me and Steve, wants to keep him a safe distance from me. But the thing about Karen's husband is—' She paused, wondering whether she should tell her aunt about her father losing half a million because of him. 'He's a bit of an enigma. Apparently, he doesn't appear to have any friends or family.'

'Well, perhaps he was orphaned or abandoned. Maybe he's a Barnardo's boy.'

Vanessa sighed deeply. 'Oh, God! I hope everything will be all right at Mum's funeral tomorrow.'

'Why wouldn't it be?'

'Because Dad's fallen out with Karen's husband. Big time. He doesn't trust him.'

'Oh? Why's that?'

'His company went bust, owing Dad half a million.'

'Huh!' Christine exclaimed harshly. 'Marcus can afford the loss. What's the big deal? He can support his son-in-law, can't he? I'm sure Paul couldn't help going bust.'

Vanessa chewed her lip thoughtfully. She had always suspected her aunt had never liked her father, though she had always kept the thought at arm's length. Now she felt it was time to learn the truth about how her

42

aunt felt about her brother-in-law. She turned the left indicator on, eased the car into the inside lane and dropped her speed.

'Can I ask you something, Aunty Christine?'

'That sounds ominous.'

'Well, yes, I...when we were in the airport car park just now, and I said I was giving you a lift to Richmond, you said you want to go to Kensington because you've booked a room at the Hilton. But there are five bedrooms at the Richmond house, four of which are empty—'

'I just need time to be alone. Get over the journey.'

'Didn't Dad offer to put you up?'

'He did. And I said I would make my own arrangements.'

'You've never liked Dad, have you?'

'What makes you say that?'

'I would have thought it was obvious. For a start, you've chosen to stay two nights at an expensive hotel instead of staying free of charge with your brother-in-law.'

There was a long pause, and a whoosh of air being displaced as a lorry overtook them. Vanessa glanced sideways and, like a brief camera snapshot, captured her aunt's image, staring at the road ahead, lost for words.

'Sorry. I shouldn't have asked you that – about Dad. It was an unfair question.'

Her aunt cleared her throat noisily, then said, 'Why *did* you ask me, Vanessa?'

'I just needed to know, that's all.' She knew how weak it sounded, and added, 'I hadn't really thought about it before now. Or if I did, I pushed it to the back of my mind.'

'Has something happened, between you and your father?'

Vanessa wanted to confide in her aunt, expose her father's infidelity, but held back, knowing how disastrous this could be prior to the funeral. The show had to run smoothly, especially as old colleagues from the world of fashion had been invited to attend.

'No, nothing,' she lied. 'It's just that whenever you came over to visit Mummy, you never had much to do with Dad. And I always felt – sort of sensed – you never liked each other. And when we came to visit you and your family in Manhattan, it was always Mummy, myself and Karen.'

'Up until five years ago,' her aunt said bitterly. 'And then it was just your mother. And I had to explain to Richard and the two boys why you and Karen wouldn't be visiting us again.'

Aware of her aunt's disapproval of her and Karen's conflict, and a reluctance to admit to disliking their father, Vanessa decided to change the subject. 'Yes, it must be over six years since we've seen Miles and Charlie. They must have grown considerably.'

'Miles is still at school, and Charlie will be going to college in just over a year's time. He's taking a gap year to travel in India and the Far East. He'll be leaving in six weeks' time.'

On hearing the tight-lipped monotone, the way her aunt conveyed this information, Vanessa tried to swing the negative into a positive.

'I'd love to see my cousins again. Especially Charlie before he leaves on his backpacking adventure. Maybe I could—'

'Come and visit?' enquired her aunt. 'I don't think you'd be very welcome.'

Vanessa was shocked, swallowed dryly, and mumbled after an impotent pause, 'Why not?' Although she could guess the reason.

'Let me put it another way, Vanessa: you and Karen would both be extremely welcome. It's what my sister would have wanted. So, when you both come to your senses and heal this ridiculous rift, that's when you will always be welcome to stay with us.'

Vanessa gripped the steering wheel tightly and felt like ramming the car in front of her, then braked sharply the last minute, conscious of her strong desire to survive, so that she could commemorate the love she had for her mother.

But there was also another reason.

Her father. She wanted him to suffer for his sordid duplicity.

*

While Vanessa drove her aunt to the Kensington Hilton, her father enjoyed a post-coital late lunch at Carluccio's in Richmond, within easy walking distance of his home.

How are you feeling, Mel?' he asked, gazing across the table with what he thought was his most alluring smile, not overdone. Mysterious yet assertive.

Melanie wondered if he meant the morning of sex or the formal engagement, so she simply shivered and said, 'Goose-pimply.'

He laughed and pointed at the large sharing board of antipasti before them. 'I hope you haven't lost your appetite. You've hardly eaten a thing. And this is our breakfast as well.'

She giggled suggestively. 'I think I had my breakfast three hours back.'

He raised his glass of champagne, and waited for her to clink glasses with him. 'Here's to mid-September,' he said. 'And our honeymoon in Barbados.'

She sipped some champagne, then picked delicately with her fingers a small sliver of salami and popped it into her mouth. She chewed and swallowed, then looked relieved as if being watched eating by Marcus was embarrassing. She laughed nervously as she said, 'For a long time we were just – I don't know – just biding our time, I suppose. And now we can please ourselves. I hope that doesn't make me sound thoughtless – you know, about the funeral and everything. There seem to be so many things happening all at once.'

She was referring to the impending non-speaking role she had in a television film and hoped Marcus might question her about it, a topic less dreary than the funeral which had been on his mind so much lately.

'Yes,' he agreed with an ironic chuckle. 'So much is and *has* been happening lately. I feel absolutely shattered. I've been going mental trying to arrange everything. And my daughters haven't exactly been much help.'

'And still you found time this morning for two hours of nookie.'

He wondered if spending the day before the funeral indulging in sex was a defiant act, or should he have been tearing his hair out with worry? Never mind. Everything was arranged. He had spent an entire day on the telephone organising, making certain the right people would be there. But he was uncertain about which music to choose, and thought about ringing Karen, but didn't trust himself not to scream and shout about her worthless husband. Three days ago, he rang Vanessa instead, wondering why he found her so uncommunicative and aloof. She told him she would think about it and promised to ring back. An hour later she gave him her music suggestions, and when he asked her if anything was wrong, other than being upset about her mother, she hung up. He then emailed both his daughters and asked them to think about writing a brief eulogy, either that or a reading of one of their mother's favourite poems.

But the important eulogy: the eulogy he would speak, was composed before Julia died. He even pictured himself at the lectern, standing tall and distinguished. Not a hint of East End now. Scene from a movie. Many in the congregation dabbing tearful eyes when he got to the bit about their eyes meeting across the crowded room during that enchanted evening.

Without thinking, he patted the breast pocket of his jacket.

'What's up?' Melanie asked. 'Have you forgotten something?'

'Just checking I've got my speech prepared. Feeling a bit nervous.'

'What time is the funeral tomorrow?' Melanie asked, with some reluctance.

He had already told her, quite a few times, and guessed she was being polite, showing concern, not wanting to look unsympathetic, selfishly thinking of her own rosy future. As he gazed across the table at her, basking in her promiscuously sensual lips and luscious figure, he realised that here was history repeating itself, but with a big difference. He was now fifty-nine and Mel was only thirty-three, whereas Julia had been only four years younger than him.

'Two p.m.,' he told her yet again. 'And then the wake is any time after three-thirty.'

She put a hand on his and squeezed. 'I hope it won't be too traumatic, darling. I expect after what you've been through – I mean, you've been expecting it for a long time, haven't you?'

He nodded and frowned, suddenly feeling a pang of guilt, though nothing too jarring. He had met Melanie over two years ago, and they had conducted the affair discreetly. Then Julia became ill, and went downhill rapidly over the last six months, and this seemed to be the answer to his prayers. Instead of a costly divorce, now he would be free as a widower to start over again with his sexy young actress.

Not that he had any illusions about her talent. She had shown him a short film she did, a film in which she had earnt the princely sum of zero. He hated to admit it, however much he fancied her, she was wooden, and even her voice lacked any passion or drive. But what did that matter now that she was about to become his stunningly attractive wife, someone to drive the guys at the golf club wild with jealousy.

'Marcus, can I ask you something?' Melanie said, pursing her lower lip petulantly, knowing he might object to what she had to say.

'Go on,' he said, helping himself to an artichoke heart and a portion of Parma ham.

46

'There'll be a few of your wife's old modelling agency people at the funeral tomorrow, won't there?'

Shaking his head, Marcus replied, 'But they were a good deal older than Julia. She was only a youngster, and she'd given up modelling by her mid-twenties.'

'So? What difference does that make?'

'So, it means, sweetheart, they'll be retired, and I know you'd like to use my wife's funeral as a networking opportunity, but—'

'But she's gone now, so what does it matter if I mingle at the do and get chatting to a few people? Who knows? I might meet one or two people who can help with my career.'

'I doubt that very much.'

'But you never know. If you don't buy a raffle ticket, as they say—'

'I know: how can you win a raffle? But this is different.'

'How is it different?'

Marcus sighed pointedly, forcefully stabbed the ham with his fork, and spoke slowly and patiently, as if addressing a child. 'This is very, very different. My wife has just died because she was riddled with cancer, and tomorrow is her funeral, and it is not a good idea for her husband's mistress to attend.'

Melanie smiled, raised her hand, showing him the ring. 'I think you mean fiancée, darling.'

'Even so,' Marcus muttered as his mouth fastened on the ham like a ravenous mongrel.

Melanie pouted again, a teasing look, designed to manipulate in a sexy manner. And it worked. Once Marcus had swallowed the ham, he looked at her and smiled. There was no getting away from it. There was something erotic about that pout. Or was he deluding himself? Was he just another old fool in love with a woman years younger than him? He dismissed the thought and scooped sun-dried tomatoes onto his plate.

'I'm sorry, sweetheart,' he said. 'It just wouldn't be right. My daughters will be there, and—'

'But it's not as if I know them,' she interrupted. 'Or vice versa.'

'Yes, but no one attending the funeral will know you. They'll start wondering about how you knew my wife.'

'Why don't you,' Melanie began, as though she had just had an idea, 'make out I'm a distant relation – distant cousin's daughter or something?'

'That means lying to so many people.'

She laughed, her eyes twinkling naughtily. 'Darling, we've been lying for two years, ever since we met. It has all been one big lie up until now. Oh, please, darling. What harm can it do?'

He stared at his plate thoughtfully for a moment, then clicked his fingers as he worked out a plan. 'Tell you what I'll do. I'll ring Malcolm Crichton up. He's one of my golfing buddies.'

Melanie threw him a quizzical look.

'Malcolm's at least fifteen years younger than me,' he explained. 'And he's met Julia a few times so it would be quite legitimate for him to come along to the wake tomorrow. Malcom's recently split up with his missus, *and* he owes me a big favour, so I'll get on the blower and ask him to partner you to the wake. You can make out you're with him just for tomorrow. How's that, as they say on the cricket green?'

Melanie grinned and blew him a kiss. 'You're brilliant, my darling.'

Her appetite returned and she began piling antipasti onto her plate.

Six

On the day of the funeral, Karen wore a black silk dress bought specially for the occasion from Harvey Nichols in Knightsbridge. Weeks ago, her mother requested that nobody wore sombre black to her funeral, and Karen, knowing how her mother had loved walking along the river, feeding and admiring the swans she adored, chose the black dress because it was patterned with swan prints, and the stylish Stella McCartney design was far from sombre. She paid for it using one of her own credit cards, putting her another £865 in debt, but having seen how much money Paul had squandered on his pipe dream of becoming a film producer, she shrugged it off as her prerogative. She was the breadwinner now; now that she had some design commissions lined up, whereas Paul....

She looked down at her black leather ankle boots. While at Harvey Nichols choosing the dress, she was almost tempted to buy the white ankle boots, the ones with the buckles and black heels, which perfectly matched the dress, and brightened it considerably, which would almost certainly have met with her mother's approval. Then she thought the better of it. Another five hundred pounds seemed hideously extravagant, and the boots she was wearing were adequate.

She stood in front of the dining room mirror, staring worriedly at her reflection. She wondered what Vanessa was wearing. Probably something from Marks & Spencer's, or even – God forbid! – Primark. And here she was, having spent almost a thousand pounds on a designer dress, but it would be her sister who looked the more stylish whatever show wore. How that rankled.

She heard Paul whistling tunelessly in the bedroom, and hoped he planned on wearing the Armani suit, a beautiful bright blue, respecting her mother's wishes for striking colours. He had other suits, grey and black, and although they had been keeping an argument-free distance lately, speaking only when necessary, she had asked him to observe her mother's desire for a drab-free funeral.

She looked at her watch. It was less than a half hour's drive to the Putney Vale Cemetery, but she was worried about traffic hold-ups. 'Paul!' she called out. 'It's time we left.'

'I'm coming,' he replied, barely disguising the irritation in his tone. She turned as he entered the living room, and gasped. He was wearing blue denims, a designer T-shirt and a black leather bomber jacket. He smiled, and in that smile she saw a perverse mixture of defiance and dominance, enjoying the power of humiliating her.

'You can't...' she began. 'You can't come to the funeral dressed like that. What the hell d'you think you're doing? When Mummy asked for her funeral to be bright and...and...'

She struggled to find the words.

His smile vanished and he shook his head seriously. 'I won't be coming to the funeral.'

'What d'you mean you won't be coming?' she yelled. 'It's my mother's funeral, and I need you to support me.'

He shrugged. 'Sorry. I have an important meeting with the backers of the movie, and a casting director we're taking on board to entice a well-known actor. Without him we don't get the backing we need. So, this meeting is vital.'

Karen chocked back a sob, determined to save her tears for the ceremony. 'You're my husband, for fuck's sake. What will people think if you don't attend my mother's funeral?'

'Let them think what they like. I'm not coming.'

'This is because of my father, isn't it? You're scared to meet him after what you've done.'

'Don't be ridiculous. That's got nothing to do with it.'

'But what do I tell people? They're bound to ask. Why isn't your husband with you? So what the fuck do I tell them?'

'Just give them my apologies and say I have an important business meeting. And stop swearing.'

Panicking, Karen looked at her watch again. 'And look at the time,' she screeched. 'If you're not going, how do I get there? It's too late to call a taxi. I'll miss my mother's funeral, thanks to you.'

Paul raised a hand. 'Calm down. I'll give you a lift. I'll drop you outside the gates. No problem. Then I'll come back here, park the car, and catch a train to London. Let's go, shall we?'

He smiled broadly. And for the first time she realised what it was about that smile. She hadn't thought about it before, but it had a definite swagger to it.

50

Seven

More than a hundred people attended the funeral. Most were in late middle age or nearing retirement. The day was reasonably warm, and it was a good day for showing off chic outfits, unencumbered by irritating overcoats. Most of Julia Bradshaw's contemporaries, who knew her as Jaybee, wore stunning outfits, although some of the women had anorexic figures. And there were many hats that wouldn't have looked out of place at Royal Ascot.

But it was what Julia, or Jaybee, had wanted.

What she hadn't wanted, however, was the continuing division of her daughters, who sat either side of their father and aunt throughout the service, Vanessa sitting next to her aunt and Karen next to her father. If anyone in the chapel noticed this division, how apart the siblings seemed to be, there were no whispered comments.

Karen, hoping her sister didn't notice, made sidelong glances in her direction. She was almost certain the dress Vanessa wore she had seen in Marks and Spencer's. It was orange, with white triangular designs, like little upside-down parachutes. And her sister looked stunning in it, in a dress which couldn't have cost more than thirty pounds. How that sent palpitations of resentment through Karen's entire system. Aware she was being small-minded, she listened to the music and tried to concentrate on thinking about her mother.

The music Vanessa had chosen was 'Cavatina', otherwise known as the theme from *The Deer Hunter*. Although her mother hated the film, she loved the music, so Vanessa chose this as a prelude to the service as the mourners entered. An organist had been hired, and during the middle of the short service the congregation stood up and sang 'All Things Bright and Beautiful', which was the only slant towards religion during the service. The eulogies followed in quick succession by Karen, Vanessa and Marcus. And then, as the coffin was carried out by professional pall bearers, a rendition of Ella Fitzgerald singing 'Manhattan'. When this was played, although there were tears in Christine's eyes, she acknowledged Vanessa's choice with a small nod of approval. Her sister had loved New York City and this number.

51

At the graveside, many mourners, those who hadn't been so close to Jaybee, respectfully held back in the circle surrounding the grave, and the interment was short and sweet with a brief prayer suitable for a non-religious service, followed by a traditional throwing on of earth when the coffin was in place. The placing of the gravestone would come later, and both Karen and Vanessa inwardly promised themselves they would visit and lay fresh flowers by the grave, both hoping they might not pick the same day to do it. Then everyone shuffled awkwardly towards the car park and Marcus took charge, giving everyone directions to the venue for the wake. The mourners relaxed. Retaining respectful grave expressions, but more animated now. Chatting about the nice weather. Good day for a funeral. Thoughts of food and drink uppermost in their minds, a comfort after the short but melancholic service.

As Karen and Christine had no transport, they were offered a lift by Marcus. Christine sat in the front passenger seat of the Jaguar, and Karen sat directly behind her father, wishing she had chosen the other side, as he could make eye contact with her in the rear view mirror, and she guessed he wanted to know about Paul's lack of attendance. The conversation during the short journey from Putney to Richmond was polite and stilted to begin with, kicked off by Marcus.

'Went quite well I thought. A surprising number of her old colleagues came, plus a few celebs from our nights out on the town when we first went out together.'

'Yes, it did go well, 'Christine admitted. 'Although it was very short.'

'It was what Julia requested. She wanted us to celebrate – drink and chat. It was her style, Christine.'

His sister-in-law remained silent, and he mistakenly assumed it was a silence of disapproval. It irritated him. Then, catching Karen's eye in the driving mirror, he saw her look away. Always on a short fuse when he thought others were ungrateful for his largesse, his irritation moved up a notch.

'So where is your husband, Karen? Why didn't he come with you?'

There was a pause while Karen wondered how to excuse Paul's lack of attendance.

'Well?' Marcus snapped.

'He's feeling ill. Got a virus or something.'

'Oh, really?' Said with a sneer in his voice. 'You don't think it's because he doesn't want to meet me because of what's happened?'

'No…I…' Karen struggled to disagree with her father.

Christine turned and gave her brother-in-law a disparaging look. 'Do you think this is an appropriate moment to bring this up? It's Julia's funeral, for God's sake.'

'Yes, I'm sorry, Christine. You're right. I just thought Paul should have been present to support his wife, that's all.'

'Maybe he's scared you'll make a scene about the money you reckon he owes you.'

'Reckon?' Marcus questioned with an ironic laugh.

Karen leant forward and stared at her aunt. 'How did you know about Dad being a guarantor for Paul's business?'

'Vanessa told me on the way back from Heathrow.'

'Vanessa told you?' Karen said, scowling at her aunt.

'Well, she must have heard it somewhere. Not from you, that's for sure, as you haven't been on speaking terms for the last five years. But does it really matter where she heard it?

Karen sighed and sat back. 'No, I suppose not.'

'Let's forget it, shall we?' Marcus offered. 'For today, at least. Let's put problems like Paul going bust onto the back burner.'

Karen nodded and was silent. She noticed her father hadn't offered to put the problems behind them and move on. Which meant he would drag them up again as soon as the funeral was a distant memory. And probably not so distant, she guessed.

*

The wake was held in one of the function rooms and bars of the London Welsh Rugby Club in Old Deer Park. Marcus had chosen the venue because it was conveniently close to Putney Vale Cemetery, and there was a good size car park. But the main reason for choosing it was because he could walk home from there, or call for a cab should he feel inebriated. He was always careful about drinking and driving these days, having suffered a year's ban when he was breathalysed driving home after dinner at The Fat Duck in Bray in 2009.

A lavish buffet was spread across two tables on one side of the room, and along another wall another table was thick with bottles of red and white wine, jugs of orange juice and mineral water. Half the guests made a beeline for food, while others headed for the alcohol.

Conversations hummed discreetly at first, but after a while, as alcohol loosened tongues, came raucous laughter, and occasional high-pitched screams of delight as funny or outrageous stories were related or recounted. Old friends and colleagues of Julia's felt duty-bound to glance at Marcus every so often, excuse themselves from a group, and come to shake his hand and offer condolences and a fond memory of his wife.

Karen latched on to two singers she vaguely knew, a boy and girl duo, for whom she had designed their vinyl album. Vanessa was at the other end of the room, and every so often Karen's eyes would dart across to where her sister stood, talking to an ageing, retired theatrical agent with multi-coloured hair and a gold lamé dress.

People were still arriving, ones who had missed the service, and many of the male drinkers went into the bar and purchased pints of beer or glasses of spirits. It was a cash bar and some of the drinkers huddled conspiratorially, bending close to bitch about Marcus Bradshaw whom they described as miserly, knowing he was probably a billionaire and could easily afford 'champers' and anything from the bar anyone wanted to drink. It was his wife they adored, and if she only knew how tight-fisted he had been over the catering…

Vanessa, talking to the retired agent, suddenly stopped in mid-sentence as a couple entered the room. She felt a stab of pain in her chest and almost dropped her wine glass.

It was her! That bitch. Her father's cheap whore. The filthy slag she'd seen at Greenwich. What the fuck was she doing here – at her mother's funeral? But Vanessa was confused. The young woman was with a well-dressed man – in his mid-forties she guessed – who had an arm round her waist. Perhaps she had been mistaken about her father. Maybe this woman was this man's girlfriend and merely one of her father's friends or colleagues. It still didn't explain the intimate behaviour she had witnessed in Greenwich.

'Is something wrong, Vanessa?' the ex-agent asked her.

As if she hadn't heard the agent, Vanessa stared at her in confusion. 'Sorry. I…I was just feeling a bit—'

The ex-agent, with a shake of her violet, cerise and yellow hair, smiled sympathetically. 'I understand. Your mother was a lovely woman. It's always hard to lose a loved one.'

But Vanessa was distracted by the arrival of the woman she'd seen with her father, and she watched as the couple made their way to the drinks table. She gave the ex-agent a nod, to show she was listening, but her eyes kept darting over to the young woman and her escort. The ex-agent, not wanting to be rude, but wanting to get away from Vanessa to talk to other people she knew, squeezed Vanessa's hand and said, 'I've just got to visit the little girl's room. Would you excuse me?' It was her excuse to get away, then when she returned she could join another group.

As Vanessa scanned the crowded room a while later, having lost sight of the young woman from Greenwich, she inadvertently caught Karen's eye. They held each other's gaze for a moment, and then Karen, as if embarrassed by this long-standing feud, looked away.

For the next hour, the twins mingled, and Karen deliberately avoided bumping into Vanessa. But Vanessa was more concerned with the puzzling behaviour of the young woman and her escort, who had abandoned each other's company not long after their arrival. As she moved slowly around the room, she heard snatches of conversation like clips from movie trailers.

A willowy blonde woman, with sunken cheeks, told a dumpy, Spanish-looking man,' Yes, my dog used to play with David Bailey's dog.' And she heard a white-haired man telling a woman with gigantic breasts, 'Organic, that's the answer. Fifty years' time the entire population will be vegans.' Then, as she passed a couple of ageing rock 'n' rollers, she heard one of them say, 'Yeah, man, that was some memorial service. They had a couple of the original skiffle group. Tea chest an' all. Can you believe that?'

Vanessa watched her father closely, who was now talking to the man who had escorted the young woman from Greenwich to the wake. Although Vanessa was quite close to them now, because of the babble of the room it was difficult to eavesdrop on their conversation. And she could have been wrong, she could have sworn she heard her father say 'blow job' loudly. She saw him looking over his shoulder, aware that someone may have heard him. The other man, clearly a friend of his, laughed, bent forward and muttered something. Vanessa stared at them, clutching her drink. Two men, sharing dirty, locker-room talk. And why, she asked herself, if her father's friend had arrived with the young woman, were they no longer in each other's company?

Her attention was distracted when she spotted the young woman quite close to her. Circulating. Clearly networking. But what Vanessa found most peculiar was the way her father totally ignored his friend or lover, whatever their relationship was. Surely if they knew one another, they would at least speak, if only briefly in passing.

Vanessa's suspicions, instead of being allayed by her father's friend accompanying the young woman to the wake, intensified as she saw her father deliberately avoiding the woman, yet she saw by the way he made eye contact with her every so often that they had some sort of relationship, and the signals that passed between them reminded Vanessa of her father's eulogy, the way he spoke of the first romantic contact with her glamorous mother, their eyes meeting across a crowded room.

An hour passed. During that hour, the twins mingled dutifully, though still managed to avoid each other. By now, many of the guests had had plenty to drink, and began hugging, air-kissing and drifting away, promising to keep in touch. Another thirty minutes went by, and there couldn't have been more than a dozen people left in the room. Karen, feeling awkward now the safety in numbers had diminished, offering less protection from her sister's searching glances, thought it was time to make a move. She went over to her aunt, and was just about to hug her and make some dutiful niece-like expression of affection, when all hell broke loose.

It happened as Melanie Martin reached the exit, accompanied by Malcolm Crichton, Marcus Bradshaw's friend. She turned and looked back at her lover. The pretence had been kept up until this fragile moment, but Vanessa spotted that look between two lovers that speaks so loudly. They might as well have been lying naked in bed together. The look said it all and Vanessa knew beyond a fraction of doubt. Her father had the barefaced audacity to bring his lover to her mother's funeral. It was an outrage.

'You bitch!' Vanessa screamed across the room. 'You fucking bitch!'

The room was stilled. Everyone froze. Had they heard correctly? Was this the drunken effect of bereavement? And then they saw Vanessa charge across the room to confront her father's fiancée, her finger pointing accusingly at the bewildered young woman, who cringed and looked desperately towards her lover.

How had this happened? She had never met Marcus's daughters. And, as far as she knew, they had no knowledge of her.

'How dare you!' Vanessa screamed in her face, so close that Melanie leaned back and staggered as she almost fell over. 'Don't try and deny you and Dad are not shagging each other. I saw you both at Greenwich three weeks ago, and just two days after Mummy died you were at Richmond. I saw you driving away. What were you doing there? Fucking my father while my mother was….'

Unable to continue, Vanessa broke down, and buried her head in her hands. Her aunt leapt forward and comforted her, while her father came striding across the room to rescue his fiancée.

'I think it best if you and Malcolm leave quickly, Melanie. Sorry about this. I'll call you later.'

They departed hurriedly, breaking through a small group of six people who watched the scene with horrified expressions.

Christine, who had never liked her brother-in-law, now looked at him with a face contorted with disgust. 'So it's true,' she said. 'You and that…that young woman have been carrying on while my sister was close to death.'

Marcus turned to face her, an animal snarl curling his lip. 'We've been carrying on for quite some time, if you must know. And she is now my fiancée, and we intend to get married.'

Karen, as she stared at her father, felt her stomach turning over and thought she might be sick. Was she losing control? And how was it her sister knew about this affair, and she didn't? Christ! Her father. She had always suspected he bent the rules and was a ruthless operator, but thought his business empire had nothing to do with family life. Now that she knew, all the things she remembered about him and the past flashed through her brain like a television show fast-forwarding.

Late nights. Excuses. Business trips abroad. Private phone calls. Evasions.

He was a swindler and a cheat. Just like her husband.

Karen stared at her father, hating him, swallowing hard to control her nausea, suddenly remembering what she had tried all these years to erase.

'OK,' Marcus yelled at the remaining six people huddled near the exit, 'the show's over. Thank you for coming. Goodbye and goodnight.'

Six mourners beat an embarrassed hasty retreat, several of them bumping into each other as they departed like a flock of frightened birds. Apart from Christine, Vanessa and Karen, the only people remaining in the room were two catering staff behind the drinks table, who stared down at the table, afraid to look up. Marcus rounded on them.

'You two! Leave us alone, will you? In other words, piss off now!'

One of the staff, a young woman in her late teens, crossed the room quickly, stifling a grin. She had witnessed what she might later describe as an 'amazing event' to her friends. Her male counterpart followed, his expression inscrutable as he passed close to Marcus, avoiding eye contact.

'Well,' Christine said after they had gone, 'we see your father in his true colours now.'

Tearfully, Karen stared at her father. 'I can't believe you were with that woman at our place just two days after Mummy died.'

'Oh!' her father sneered. 'Our place, is it? Well, not any more. And Melanie will be moving in with me in about eight weeks' time. I accept we need to keep a bit of decorum about the arrangement, just to keep all the hypocritical little prigs in life happy.'

Vanessa took her hands away from her face, wiped her eyes and glared at her father. 'You really plan to marry that little scrubber?'

'Just over three months away,' he answered with a slightly smug smile. 'The date's already set for the second week in September.'

'She must be half your age,' Christine pointed out.

'Not quite. But close.' His grin widened now he felt he was regaining control of the situation. 'Nice work if you can get it.'

'You're disgusting,' Karen said. 'How long have you been...been having an affair with that woman?'

'Must be going on for two years now.'

Christine felt like slapping her brother-in-law. Tight-lipped, she said, 'So my sister's death was very convenient, wasn't it? Had you split up with Julia, it would have cost you in alimony.'

Marcus wanted to reply, tell her how fortunate that was, but even he knew there were certain things that were better left unspoken. He merely shrugged, which infuriated Christine.

'And what about Vanessa and Karen?'

'What about them?'

'If you marry that woman—'

'She'll be entitled to my estate,' he interrupted, 'if anything should happen to me. Is that what you were going to say?'

'Something like that. So I hope you'll have the decency to make a proper will, and leave at least two thirds to your daughters.'

'Will I fuck!'

Shocked, Christine stepped back, as if he had struck her in the face. 'What did you say?'

'They were both spoilt as children. They had everything they needed from when they were born. Never had to struggle. They both had an expensive private education, then university for the business woman who can't run a fucking sandwich bar, and art school for the one who marries a pathetic little turd who pretends he's a great entrepreneur. Hah! He'd got booted off on day one by Lord Sugar. I gave them the deposit for a sprauncy flat in Kingston, and how does the little wanker repay me? By robbing me of half a million quid.'

'Money you can well afford,' Christine said.

'That's not the point, is it? I had to work hard to achieve my success. It doesn't come easy, you know.'

Vanessa sighed loudly and pointedly. 'Oh, not that old cliché we've heard a million times. No pain, no gain.'

Her belittling him in this way angered him, and he yelled, 'What would you know about it? A degree in business studies just to butter bread. And still you can't make a go of it. I've given both of you all that you deserve. As far as I'm concerned, you are both grown up enough to sort your own financial messes out. That's life. That's how it is for most people who never had your opportunities.'

'You're forgetting something important here,' Christine said, coldly and calmly. 'Something you've left out of your nasty, self-centred, egotistical, self-regarding history. However much trouble Karen and Vanessa have got themselves into financially, it shouldn't just be a father's duty to help them out. It should be done out of love. You seem incapable of that emotion. You know what. You are a typical psychopath. Oh, you might not have physically murdered anyone, but you have metaphorically killed your children. You have the psychopath gene in you, and it's something I always suspected.'

Marcus stared at his sister-in-law with such venom, such hatred, that his daughters feared for their aunt's safety. The hiatus lasted for what seemed a long time, but was only a few seconds, and Christine appeared unfazed by his malevolent stare, though it took her an enormous amount of self-control. Then Marcus smiled, and she saw something in his eyes that signalled his comeback would be blunt and cruel.

'I couldn't give a shit about what you think. Never have done; never will. And now that Julia's dead, you can fuck off into the sunset.' He directed his malicious glare towards Karen. 'As for your husband, you can tell him from me that I will be gunning for him. I don't suppose he's got a pot to piss in now, so don't think you can come running back to Richmond when you have to abandon that flat in Kingston, because Melanie will be moving in with me.'

And then, satisfied with having dealt with one of his daughters, he turned his attention to Vanessa. 'As for you, turning your mother's funeral into a farce. You have no one to blame but yourself. If you wanted to make a scene, you should have waited till all the guests left.'

Vanessa's eyes widened with disbelief. 'You hypocrite. It's your fault for bringing that little slag to Mummy's funeral.'

'She wasn't at the service. So what?'

'And even on the day Mummy died you were on the phone to that woman, weren't you?' Karen yelled. 'We heard you. She'd been dead less than an hour and you were arranging to book the train to Paris.'

Marcus shrugged. 'Life has to move on. And that's only a week's holiday for us on the second week in June.'

'You know something?' Vanessa hissed. 'Even as a little girl I never liked you. Never. Especially as—' She stopped speaking abruptly, scared of the way her father stared at her with such malevolence. She swallowed rapidly several times and changed direction. 'This is all about you being jealous, isn't it?'

'Jealous? What are you on about?'

'Because of our love for Mummy. You couldn't stand it, could you? The way we loved her and looked up to her. Knowing she was a much better person than you. And knowing how much we loved her and never liked you.'

'You're talking bollocks.'

'Maybe you're right. Because it's not that I don't like you anymore. I hate you. I really hate you and wish you were dead.'

Marcus smiled thinly. 'Well, if what you wish comes true, you'd better be quick. Cos the wedding's just over three months away. And when Mel and I are married – who knows – she might become pregnant. She might give me a son. I'd like a boy, especially as my daughters have been such a big disappointment.'

Karen laughed bitterly. 'He thinks he's like royalty. Must have a male heir.'

Marcus pursed his lips, looked at all three of them, then said, 'I think we're all done here.' Turned and exited sharply.

'Another cliché,' Vanessa called after him. 'Bad TV cop show. Fucking bastard!'

She stared at her father's retreating form, striding purposefully through the adjoining bar, watched by the bar staff. She hated him. But she felt so utterly helpless, wanting to hurt him, to get back at him, but could think of no way of retaliating for the dishonourable way he had treated their mother.

Karen, tears running freely down her face, said, 'I hate him too. And I wish he was dead.'

Her aunt, having spent most of the furore comforting Vanessa, decided it was time to give some comfort to Karen. She was about to slip away from Vanessa and go over to her other niece when an older man entered.

'If you're all finished here,' he enquired tentatively, 'do you mind if we start to clear up?'

Eight

Karen had never felt so miserable in all her life. She sat in the lounge of their spacious flat staring into space, swallowed up by the ostentatious sofa. She suddenly hated everything about the flat, and wouldn't care where they ended up. Even a bedsit in Deptford. What did it matter? Not that she had ever been to Deptford, but she vaguely knew something about the district. Hadn't Christopher Marlowe been stabbed there more than 400 years ago?

She looked at her watch, wondering where Paul had got to. It was gone nine o'clock and she felt numbed by the flat's silence. All she could hear was a strange buzzing in her ears, and an occasional car revving up Kingston Hill or the roar of a motorcycle. She wanted to get up and pour herself a gin and tonic but remained seated, depressed and dry-eyed. She had wept bitterly after she returned home at seven-thirty, but now all she felt was an ache deep inside, an emptiness which she knew was a longing to be with her mother once more.

Now her family had totally disintegrated, torn apart by their father, and she knew there would never be a remedy to heal the deep division caused by his selfish acts. Although it was Vanessa who had to shoulder a hefty portion of the blame because of the affair with Steve, but nothing back then was as bad as this, now that her mother was gone. And what did her father mean by saying he was out to get Paul? What could he do to him? Standing as a guarantor for Paul's business didn't mean he could take it any further. Maybe it was said in the heat of the moment. Though she doubted it. From what she had seen of her father today, and the things he said, she knew damn well there was nothing he wouldn't do to take his revenge on Paul.

God! *How she hated her father. Her hatred consuming her like her mother's cancer.*

And was Paul so very bad? Perhaps she was wrong to think he was like her father. He was naïve, often lacking in sense, but at least he wasn't as devious as her father. His major fault was that he acted bigger and better than he was, and made some very stupid decisions.

Like this scheme to produce a gangster film. But what if it came off? What if Paul, the great pretender, did hit it big. That would show her father, and she pictured herself laughing at him.

Then she heard the key in the door. He was home. Perhaps he had some good news about the film. She hoped, prayed, for the only light in the darkness of that day, the only possible liberating event following the nightmare scene with her father.

She held her breath as the lounge door opened and Paul entered. And her hopes suddenly plummeted when she saw the heavy dejection of his shoulders. The pretender no longer pretending as he slumped into the easy chair, and sat with a hand covering his forehead and eyes.

Now the day would end on a note of utter defeat. She felt like screaming. Wanted to bang her head against the wall. Pain to stop the pain. And as she watched her husband – who didn't even have the guts to look at her – her mood changed. The recent character of her father surfaced and, like a cat flexing its claws ready to toy with its prey, she spoke calmly with a voice frozen with malice.

'I suppose it's *another* failure. Another stupid pie-in-the-sky scheme gone down the pan.'

He took his hand away from his eyes, and she saw they were bloodshot. At first she thought it might be because he'd been crying, but his slurred speech told her he was drunk.

'Gloat if you like. Go on and gloat. Even if it is through your stupid mixed metaphors.'

Her anger rushed to the surface. 'I might mix my metaphors,' she shouted, 'but at least I have some grasp on reality. Not some…some…stupid pretence. That's what your life is. You're living a lie. It's time you faced up to—'

Pointing his finger at her, he interrupted with, 'What do you know? You just don't understand, tha's all. Admittedly it's a setback, but it's not a total disaster. The backers thought they were getting Ray Winstone but we can't even get him to read the script. And without a leading actor in place, they're not interested. So we'll just have to find someone else.'

'And that's going to be easy, is it?'

'What do you know about it?'

'I know enough to realise most stars want to work for reputable companies, not for unknown producers who can't even run a small travel agency without going bust. You do realise, we might have to sell this flat.'

63

Paul waved his hand in the air, like he didn't care. 'We'll just downsize, tha's all.'

'That's if you haven't borrowed again on the flat.'

'Of course I haven't. Don't worry. There'll be plenty of equity on it. Providing that miserly billionaire doesn't want his deposit back.'

'That deposit was a wedding present. Anyway, I don't think I'll be seeing my father from now on.'

Paul stared at her uncomprehendingly, his forehead screwed up in confusion. 'Oh, I suppose he's still pissed off about the guarantee business for the agency.'

'Yes, he is still pissed off about that. And he said he's going to come after you. Gunning for you, he said.'

Paul snorted. 'What can he do? He was a guarantor. The money's gone. Kaput. Tha's that!'

'I got the impression he was going to get you in another way.'

'What other way? What are you talking about?'

'I've no idea. I'm just telling you what he said. And now I know how ruthless he can be. He's a one-hundred per cent bastard and he's out to get you.'

As Karen watched her husband, she saw a change come over him. Whereas a moment ago he had been like most men having had too much to drink, suddenly there was a look in his eyes like that of a cornered animal, both cunning and desperate.

'I need a drink,' he said.

'I should think you've had enough.'

He struggled to stand up. 'I think I'll pop down to the Albert Arms for a few beers.' He fumbled in his pockets, swaying slightly, took out his wallet, opened it, and saw there was no money in it. 'Trouble is, I think I've run out of—' His eyes roamed around the room and eventually latched on to Karen's handbag by the side of the sofa. He staggered across the room to it, but she snatched it away.

'No, you don't,' she said.

He grabbed the bag and tugged. They struggled for a moment, and then he suddenly lashed out, hitting her hard across the face with his open palm. She shrank back onto the sofa, crying and frightened as he tipped the contents of her bag onto the coffee table. He opened her purse and took out the only twenty pound note that was in there.

After she heard the door slam, she dried her eyes and picked up the cordless phone. She held it for a long time without dialling, not even sure if she could remember the number. And then, after pouring herself that gin and tonic, she dialled the number.

Nine

Three months after Jenny's funeral, I was still waiting for her estate to be settled. She had died intestate, and the wheels of bureaucracy turn slowly. During that stagnant period, I took to studying an atlas of Great Britain, looking for a town or city of reasonable size. I realised my mistake in trying to run a PR company in a city the size of Aberdeen had only added to my difficulties as an ambitious entrepreneur simply because of the competition from longer-established residents. That was when I discovered Bangor in North Wales. Perfect. One of the smallest cities in the UK, a population of less than 20,000, with a huge catchment area and probably not many public relations firms.

It took six months for Jenny's estate to finally resolve itself into my impatiently-waiting bank account. After deductions, her savings amounted to a grand total of just over ten-thousand pounds. Far less than I expected, but then my PR company had swallowed up quite a bit until she screamed her objections, resulting in her fatal accident.

The house, though, needed a lot of work done on it, and fetched less than a quarter of a million. I wound up the company, and the sale of the Saab went a little way to paying for minor things like outstanding utility bills. My two employees got exactly what was owed to them, no more no less. Because I had no intention of ever returning to that part of the world, I could have done a bunk, but I needed to leave Aberdeen without leaving a trail behind, vanishing into the future to seek my fortune, heading south in my Range Rover, with almost no possessions. Who needs much in the way of material things when you have a bank balance of two-hundred grand? Not a vast fortune, admittedly, but enough for a fresh start.

Eighteen months after Jenny's unfortunate accident, I arrived in Bangor, ready to take over that bijou city like an occupying force. Grab it. Conquer it. Mould it. Of course, I realised I was setting myself up as a big fish in a small pond, but each thousand miles starts with one step.

I had been in Bangor less than a month when I discovered what a close-knit community it was, with a couple of well-established PR companies hogging the limelight. Planning to swallow up those little fish, I soon sussed out that what I needed in this tiny but thriving city were a couple of employees who spoke the language like natives. Having done my research, I found out that more than fifty per cent of the population in that part of the world spoke Welsh, so I began listening to Welsh language CDs and picked up a few phrases. Most of the natives, I reasoned, would know I was English, but if I gave them my best smile and chucked in a few phrases, I thought I could win them over.

To save money, I found a large unfurnished house to rent, up near the university, and used the ground floor as office space, with the upstairs as my living accommodation. I had been in Bangor for well over six months when I advertised for two fluent Welsh speakers, a female to run the office and a male employee to assist me and translate when necessary. After a week of job interviews, I ended up employing Gareth, a bloke in his early-thirties, and Cheryl, an attractive young woman in her mid-twenties.

I named the business Dragon PR and we began touting for business. But after nearly three months – Zilch. A big fat nothing. And I was now paying the salary of two employees, plus my own living expenses, with my bank balance dwindling fast. Gareth and Cheryl, at their job interview, gave me the impression that with their connections and local contacts, we'd soon be rolling in it. When I reminded them of that fact, they evaded the issue, and we had a heavy argument about it. Things began to sour. Not helped by them speaking Welsh to each other in my presence. I sensed they were talking about me. Of course, they denied it when I confronted them, but I didn't believe it for one minute.

During this unproductive period in the world of PR bullshit, I scanned the local papers for anything of interest. Mainly the obituary columns, to see if there were any impressionable widows who might like to invest in an ongoing concern. But what caught my eye was on the front page of the *North Wales Chronicle*. A woman's husband had committed suicide. He was bi-polar, and his depression eventually got to him, and no one could really explain why it was he had ended his life by drowning in the Menai Straits. I followed the story intently, which went on for many weeks as his wife, Donna Gower, contested the suicide accusations, wanting the coroner to reach a verdict of death by misadventure. She claimed that even though he had depressive moods, he could manage them when he swam long distances, occasionally liberating himself from bouts of depression by swimming across the Menai Straits from Y Felinheli Menai Marina to Anglesey. She claimed he was a strong swimmer, as she was herself, and they often swam across the Straits together. But there were suspicious circumstances, suggesting he had taken his own life. This time he had swum on his own, late in the evening, and set off from between the Britannia Bridge and the Menai Bridge, where there are dangerous currents and sometimes a whirlpool near the rocks, depending on the tides. And he swam at high tide, one of the worst possible times, when even boats are warned from navigating those waters. But his wife claimed the swim would have been a challenge to someone like her husband.

To use an old courtroom quote: she would say that, wouldn't she? Insurance companies do not pay out on suicides.

The story was big news in Bangor, and during the hearing witnesses testified that they heard her husband on several occasions saying he enjoyed wild swimming the Menai Straits, and was even tempted to swim from Y Felinheli to Holyhead along the west coast of Anglesey to raise money for charity.

After hearing this sort of evidence, the coroner's court reached a verdict of death by misadventure, which meant the probability of a juicy life insurance pay-out. Not only that, the widow was the sole owner of a small business, with no hubby to help her run it.

It was time I abandoned the bullshitty PR business, I thought, and moved on to something more stable. First, I had to allow the dust to settle. Not for too long though, in case some other dude went sniffing around, hoping to dip his wick in the widow and pocket a wad of dough.

I asked Cheryl about Y Felinheli, inadvertently mispronouncing the 'F'. She explained that there is no V in the Welsh alphabet, and an F on its own is pronounced as a V. Then she gave me a brief history of the area, which was known by the English name of Port Dinorwic.

As in many parts of North Wales, slate was mined in a quarry nearby, a harbour was built in Port Dinorwic to export the slate, and a narrow-gauge railway transported the slate down to the Menai Straits. But the little railway had long-since vanished and in recent years the harbour became the Menai Marina, an area of recreation rather than hard graft.

I liked the sound of it and looked forward to acquainting myself with the marina, but more importantly with the grieving widow. I figured she must have reached saturation point in having to suffer hubby's misery for all those years, and might soon be ready for some light relief. And there had been no mention of children in the newspaper reports, so things were looking good. Take it nice and easy, I told myself. No rush. Softly, softly, catchee monkey.

We had a couple of small jobs at Dragon PR – nothing to write home about, so I left Gareth and Cheryl to get on with it while I spent some time reconnoitring the Menai Marina.

I didn't want to make enquiries about her from any of the locals, which might arouse suspicion, so I just drifted around Y Felinheli and the marina, acquainting myself with the area.

The houses in the village itself varied from small terrace houses running down to the water's edge by the straits, to some much larger houses above the main street in the village. The district, I had to admit, was atmospheric, with typical seaside dwellings painted in pastel shades, marine engineering workshops, yacht brokers, and places offering sailing lessons. The marina was crowded with berthed yachts, making me wonder how anyone wanting to sail managed to squeeze their craft out of the congestion. There was a small drawbridge going over from the village to the marina, and there were some attractive houses on the marina itself, painted a dazzling white. The view across the straits was a picture postcard shot, and my heart quickened. I began to feel horny as I dreamed about living off the susceptible widow, moulding her and controlling her, while I indulged in life's little luxuries. Maybe, I thought, I had found my Shangri-La. Everything about the area seemed perfect. Picturesque. Mind you, it was a flawless summer, so I was under no illusions that it might well be a dead and alive hole in the winter, with sodden leaves gusting about and the wind whistling up the straits and freezing your bollocks off. Which would be the time to fly south like the birds to a more equable climate.

More than just a dream. A plan. And it wasn't long before I put it into operation.

First I researched my target, getting most of my info from the newspapers, whose story about her gloomy husband had been well documented and extensive, and I discovered their business was exporting exclusive Welsh produce to upmarket stores in Britain. Fancy cheeses, unusual liqueurs, and all kinds of crap that gullible arseholes buy to make them feel a cut above their chav neighbours. And all this produce was branded with cute cartoons of Welsh dragons and called Rugged Mountain Products. The small company was based in Caernarfon and the widow was now the sole owner and occupant of one of the biggest houses in Felinheli.

Getting the information was the easy part. The hardest part would be in attracting a recently bereaved woman. But, like I said, this one had endured his misery for many years, so I figured she was ripe for plucking.

And I was right. It turned out to be easier than I had first thought. Just like that stupid cow Jenny. Vulnerable. At a low ebb but seeing a glimmer of hope on the not so distant horizon.

I decided to keep my PR company going for at least another year or more. That way I could disappear on business whenever the fancy took me. Then, only four weeks after dour hubby had shuffled off into his watery grave, I telephoned her business premises one bright sunny Monday, guessing her weekend may have been lonely without her dearest, even if he was a miserable dickhead. I asked if we could meet; told her my PR company wanted to place a massive order for some of her produce, and what could she recommend. Well, the long and the short of it was that I ended up buying six hundred quid's worth of cheese which I dumped in the straits one night. Wasteful, I know, but the purchase was my intro to Rugged Mountain Products, and you must speculate, as they say. With my breezy charm, understanding and fake sincerity, she was a pushover. Within six months we were married.

Auburn-haired Donna, I discovered early on in our relationship, was English, despite her Celtic looks. While not exactly overweight, she was broad-shouldered and rounded – which may have been something to do with her excessive swimming – and her thighs were sturdy, but with surprisingly small breasts for someone so well-proportioned. The fact that she came from England, from somewhere in Kent to be precise, was a bonus. It meant that relatives and old friends and acquaintances lived hundreds of miles from Y Felinheli, and visits would be scarce. Another bonus was the fact that she was unable to have children, a fact which may have contributed to late hubby's depressive decline. More fool him, I thought, but turned on the sympathy when she told me.

Although I had initially thought of our relationship as a temporary solution to my economic objectives, what I hadn't really considered was that I would fall for Donna. Not love exactly – I leave that for dead poets and silly pop songs – but a kind of tranquillity, a satisfaction that I had found what I had been looking for. Of course, I realised it was partly to do with the location, and the fact that her house was comfortable and furnished in good taste, and not as fussy as I imagined it was going to be. And I fucked her regularly, enjoying the trip, especially as she was unlikely to bring a litter of bawling brats into the world. But I always kept my mind free from overwhelming passion with a degree of self-restraint. Otherwise they possess you. And I vowed that would never happen. I

70

could enjoy fucking her without ever losing control. Things were good. In fact, more than good. But there is always something to bring you crashing back down to earth.

That proverbial fly in the ointment. Dead hubby's sister, Mary, who was now close friends with the sister-in-law.

I knew the bitch didn't trust me. The way she questioned me about my PR firm, sniffing around suspiciously, doubting every reply I gave. Oh, she was subtle, I had to admit. Probing away innocently, as if she was interested in me. And Donna never suspected a thing. Why would she? But I could tell the sister-bitch smelt a rat from the way she looked at me. It was as if we could read each other's minds. Her suspicions must have been animal instinct because I had never given her any reason not to trust me. I could tell she doubted my sincerity, even though I hadn't given her any cause to distrust me.

And when the winter came, and Y Felinheli became arse-paralyzingly grey and boring, my excuses to take business trips to London were always questioned by her like some sort of third degree, so much so that I wanted to kick her stupid, four-eyed face in. She was a librarian, and had probably read too many romantic novels about underhanded men. If only she knew, I thought, what I could do to her. No qualms at all about murdering the bitch if she got in my way.

I'm ashamed to admit that on a couple of occasions I imagined strangling her, squeezing my fingers round her scrawny neck, tighter and tighter. Not that I would have felt any remorse from killing the bitch. Far from it. No, when I say I felt shame, it wasn't from the notion of strangling her. It was because it gave me a hard-on.

I soon wiped those thoughts from my mind. No way was I a pervert. I knew I must never lose control. Those thoughts can take you over, destroy the rational being. Despite wanting to murder the rancid little cunt, I tolerated her interrogations with good humour and a handy smile. This, I noticed, was the way to rile the bitch. And it also meant that as far as Donna was concerned, I was always the charming blue-eyed boy.

And then two years after we were married things started to go wrong. The PR company was losing money hand over fist. The inheritance from Jenny's estate was spent. And Donna became cautious and tight fisted and refused a loan from her company to bail out Dragon PR. She suggested I wind up the company and work alongside her at Rugged Mountain Products.

Reluctantly, I agreed. Her two employees, Bethan and Julie, were middle-aged, local women, and I detected a certain resentment that I was the boss's husband, and could change the status quo. That was when my life shifted into a low gear. A deadly crawl. I hated the fact that Donna was really the boss, and her work suggestions seemed harsh, although I guess she was merely instructing me in the way of her business. But I hated it, and usually drank in Caernarfon pubs on my own during lunchtime. Then back late from lunch. My timekeeping was shit but I didn't care. And my fuse got shorter and shorter as I resented the way Donna spoke to me in front of the staff. She had turned into a shrewish nag. But I always kept my cool. Never let my anger surface. Never lost control.

It was time to make plans.

I had been in Bangor for nearly four and a half years, and I tolerated Donna's diatribes about my tardiness and lack of interest in her business for the next six months. As far as our domestic life was concerned, I showed myself to be the model husband. Wherever we went on the marina, I always held her hand as we walked along, stopping occasionally to give her a peck on the cheek. As puke-making as I found this – reminding me of my mother and father - I wanted every local person to see how attentive and loving I was. The perfect couple.

Even her bitch sister-in-law was taken in by this demonstration of deep affection, and I could have sworn she looked at me with a mixture of guilt and confusion. She still wasn't sure and, when she was in our company, I inflated the part of doting husband. Everywhere I went with Donna, people saw two devoted lovers.

In late April, more than three weeks after an early Easter, we had some unseasonably hot weather, and although Donna often swam long distances most weekends, I suggested we took a week's annual leave to enjoy boating and swimming. And she bought it. She liked the idea of swimming this early in the year at weekdays when the water was less busy with pleasure craft. The plan was working, and I felt exhilarated, powerful and intelligent. Because that's what it was about. Not just about having the balls to carry out an audacious scheme, but in having the sharpness and brilliance to weigh up all the risks.

Another excellent detail in my plan was in taking Donna to one of the local pubs, then speaking to her in hushed tones, warning her about my concerns, the strong currents in the straits, and what happened to her husband. I mentioned it several times, and I was certain some of the regulars overheard most of our conversation, especially when Donna said that she knew I was concerned but had no intention of swimming between the bridges, and she had swum from Y Felinheli to Anglesey and back many times. Following these conversations, I invariably showed great affection by kissing her lightly, and exiting the pub with my arm round her.

My main worry was her two employees, who could always testify that we didn't get on so well at work. So, for weeks prior to our annual holiday, I made every effort to labour like I was truly interested in Rugged Mountain's poxy produce. No more pub lunches either, and the turned-a-new-leaf man took a special interest in her two workers, hoping my recent slapdash conduct might be obliterated by my energetic activity and charm. Every time I rewarded them with a smile, I got a kick out of thinking: *little do you two bitches know you'll soon be out of a job.*

Then there was that cow of her sister-in-law to consider. But since I'd devised my plan of showing so much public affection towards my wife, as if my love grew stronger every day, I soon had the ratbag eating out of my hand. Nothing too over the top in case it aroused her suspicion.

The weekend before the week's holiday, I felt excitement rising inside me as I anticipated the Monday. I had chosen Monday because Easter was well out of the way and the tourist season hadn't kicked off yet, so I didn't think there would be many visitors on the remote Anglesey side of the straits. I didn't want to risk someone randomly looking through binoculars. As Donna had a whole week in which to enjoy swimming, I persuaded her to spend Saturday visiting some tourist sites which I had yet to visit. We took a trip to Beaumaris and strolled around the castle. I had bought a small camera, and asked someone to take a photograph of us together. More evidence of the perfect couple, captured for the newspapers, adding zest to a tragic story.

We spent the rest of the weekend eating and drinking, taking things easy, while I made certain we were observed on the marina as lovers with eyes only for each other. And the anticipation of what I was about to do on the Monday was like a fire burning inside me, so that I felt I might spontaneously combust.

On Sunday night, I had to down a few brandies, knowing I would find it hard to sleep. Eventually I drifted into one of those half-sleeping states where reality blurs at the edges and you are never sure whether the images floating in your brain are part of your consciousness or your imagination.

Donna owned a small boat, a launch with a tiny single cabin under a protective windscreen, which I had been out in several times. I thought she would have been more interested in sailing, but she told me her preference was for wild swimming not boating, and the launch was simply because she and hubby happened to live near the marina and could afford to own and moor it. Because I told her I was not a strong swimmer, which wasn't a million miles from the truth, we agreed that I would take the launch out into the straits, and she could swim from there, while I relaxed, enjoying the tranquillity of the waters.

As we set off into the straits, she asked me why I was smiling. I told her it was simply because I was happy. Naturally I didn't confess to my imagination overload, picturing everything like a scene from a film. An art house movie. Poetic even. I imagined phrases like sun dappled water, warm flowing currents, and all that bollocks. A movie camera zooming in and picking out bubbles beneath the surface. The struggle for survival.

Another reason I smiled. It was early in the day and, so far, we were the only boat out in the straits. My greatest fear was if some nosy bastard on the shore watched us through binoculars or a telescope. Nothing I could do about that. Except keep the boat idling side on to the shore, so that Donna would go over on the Anglesey side and couldn't be seen from the marina.

I cut the engine as Donna went over the side. Quickly, I leant over the side, knowing she would tread water alongside the boat for a moment, while she said goodbye to me as she usually did before setting out for her swim.

But not today.

Today would be different.

I asked her about underwater swimming. She frowned, and I could see she was puzzled by my question. She wanted to know why I asked, and told me she was a serious wild swimmer and not really interested in underwater swimming. I explained to her that although I wasn't a strong swimmer, I had always wanted to swim beneath the surface. I mentioned the difficulty of breathing. After we think we are out of breath, how many seconds of reserve have we got left? I asked her. We put it to the test. I demonstrated expelling my breath completely, so that my lungs were empty, and she counted the seconds. I managed to hold out for around twenty-five.

My face above hers was only about a foot away, and my arms were stretched out along the boat's wooden side. She had one hand on the boat, but I could see she was keeping afloat by treading water.

Then I challenged her to a quick competition, see how many seconds she could last after emptying her lungs. I knew she was competitive and this was an irresistible challenge.

She let her breath out, blowing hard, as if she wanted to end the game quickly so that she might win and get on with her swim. I counted to almost thirty, and could see she was struggling and about to breathe in again as her lungs struggled to hold out.

That was when I grabbed her head in both hands and pushed her under the water. I held it tight. There was almost no struggle and I thought I heard a snort as she breathed in water. No reserve breath. No strength left. I could feel the struggle for survival beneath my hands, and it felt good. I was in control. There was no way she would overpower me.

But then, in a final moment of survival, I felt her head pushing against my hands and it rose above the surface, her mouth gasping for breath and spluttering. But she was too weak now and I pushed with all my might, transferring my hands to her shoulders, pinching them tight with my claw-like fingers. I could hear the bubbles and the foaming terror of her drowning, and I held her tight under the water for what seemed like minutes.

Her struggle almost over, I leaned right over the edge of the boat, fell on top of her, still holding her shoulders and pushing down and down. Eventually, I felt her body cease its struggle to survive. It was over. Now it was time to panic and cry out for my darling wife who may have got cramp.

If I had been a stronger swimmer I might have been able to save my sweetheart.

If only she had listened to my warnings about swimming the straits.

I thrashed about, crying for help, while her useless body floated away.

Ten

Two days after the funeral, Vanessa received a letter from Cranby Properties, the landlords of the sandwich bar. Their name was emblazoned across the bottom of the envelope and something told her this was not going to be good news. She picked it up off the mat in the hall, took it into the living room, placed her handbag and mobile phone on the pine table by the window, then peeled open the letter. Her eyes darted to and fro as she scanned the contents, confirming what she had suspected as soon as she saw who it was from.

Bastards! Fucking bastards!

They gave her two months' notice to vacate the premises. No reason was given, other than they were exercising their rights as stated in the terms of the agreement.

She stared at the letter for a long time. Almost uncomprehendingly. What a thing to come home to after a hectic day. And it wasn't as if she had defaulted on the rent. She always made certain the rent for the sandwich bar was paid over and above anything else.

The letter shook in her hands. She trembled with shock but no tears blurred her vision. Not this time. This time it was a numbing and deadly anger, freeing her from self-pity, as she discerned the purpose of the letter. It was revenge. The notice to quit was no coincidence. It had been sent the day after the funeral. The day after she exposed her father as a liar and a cheat.

She stared with revulsion at the letterhead, hating every partner and associate of her father's. Scum, the lot of them.

She grabbed her mobile, clicked on Contacts, and rang her father's number. It rang for a long time and she thought he might ignore it. He would have known who was ringing because her name and number would be in his list of contacts. If it switched to voice mail she wondered whether to leave a message or not. She decided against it, and was about to hang up when it was answered.

'Yes?' was all he said.

'It's Vanessa,' she announced, and waited for his response.

76

Silence. What the hell was he playing at? Was this some one-upmanship bullshit he used in his dodgy practices? She was still his daughter, for fuck's sake. But then her father had always been a distant figure. As distant as seeing him through the wrong end of a telescope; but still able to recognise the monster at the other end.

'I've just had a letter from Cranby Properties giving me notice to quit,' she said, restrained anger in her tone.

'What's that got to do with me?' he replied.

'You know fucking well what it has to do with you. Cranby Properties is one of your companies.'

'And they are almost autonomous. Make their own decisions. Often without consulting me.'

'They want me out of the sandwich bar in two months' time. For no fucking reason. It's not like I owe them any money. The direct debit's always been honoured.'

She heard him sighing pointedly.

'At the risk of repeating myself: what has this got to do with me?'

'I'll tell you what it has to do with you,' she snapped, her voice rising. 'It's still one of your companies, and you could tell them to stop what they're doing. But you want to know what I think?'

'What's that?'

'That letter was posted yesterday. The day after Mummy's funeral. This is your revenge, isn't it? Because of me having a go at your precious little bitch at the rugby club.'

'Well, face it: your behaviour was unforgiveable. If you had something to say about Melanie, you should have said it to me in private.'

'It was your fucking fault for inviting her to the funeral. Jesus Christ! I can't believe you did that.'

'She didn't come to the funeral. She came to the do afterwards.'

'Yes, and you didn't know I'd seen you together, did you? You thought you could get away with it and nobody would notice. You didn't expect anyone to make a scene about it, did you? Huh! I bet that surprised you. And that's why you've instructed Cranby Properties to terminate my tenancy. So now what the fuck do I do with no sandwich bar to run?'

'Do what most adults of your age do. Get a job. Not everyone has rich parents to help them. Now you can find out what the rest of the great unwashed go through to earn a crust. As I had to.'

77

'Oh, not that old cliché about pulling yourself up by your bootstraps and—'

She stopped speaking when she realised she was talking to a dead line. The bastard had hung up.

She hurled her mobile across the room, but made certain its target was the sofa.

*

Karen looked round as Paul entered. A broad smile on his face. A mug of coffee in his hand. He placed it carefully on the desk next to her laptop, then stood behind her, his hands on her shoulders, gentle and caressing as he stared at the images she had created on the screen.

'What's that?' he whispered. 'It looks like a sixties flower-power design.'

'That's exactly what it is. It's for a fashion magazine.'

'Do they pay well?'

'Well, considering this will only take me an hour – yes, I suppose two-hundred quid isn't bad.'

'You're very talented, my sweetheart. And I really love you, you know.' He kissed her cheek. 'I'm so sorry for what happened the other night. I didn't mean to hit you. I'll never ever do that again. I promise. It's just that I was under so much pressure.'

She wanted to say that attending her mother's funeral hadn't been exactly free from distress but remained silent.

'That was selfish of me, I know,' he said, correctly interpreting her silence. 'Your mother's funeral must have been awful.'

She brought her right hand up from the keyboard diagonally, placed it on his left hand and squeezed. 'Thank you for the coffee. Now let me get on with finishing this commission. It'll only take me another twenty minutes. If that.'

'I love those swirling orchid-like flowers, especially the colours. Brilliant.'

She smiled, and watched as he went to the door, waiting for his pose. He turned, framed in the doorway like a picture. Grinning. Cocky and sure of himself now his confidence had returned.

'There's a new Italian restaurant just opened, within walking distance. After I've put the flat on the market, I'll book us a table for tonight.' He

78

laughed as he saw the shocked expression on her face. 'Oh, come on, Karen. A final fling before we tighten our belts. And this flat'll fetch a fair price. There'll be plenty of equity there, especially as your old man gave us a generous deposit. So, if we downsize, we'll probably have a few bob left over.'

'But we'll still need a deposit for another flat,' she protested. 'And we might not find it easy to get a mortgage seeing as your business has gone bust. We'll probably need something like a thirty per cent deposit for a modest flat in a poor area.'

He sniggered. 'Let's cross that bridge when we come to it, shall we?'

He turned and left, leaving the door open. She heard him whistling happily as he walked along the hall, and then the front door closed. She stared at the screen, and found it difficult to concentrate. All she could think about was her husband, and their situation. She had wanted to confide in him – tell him about the terrible scene between her father and sister – but something told her to hold back. She trusted Paul less than ever now, and determined to keep any family problems to herself.

*

Distracted in his lovemaking with Melanie both at night and the attempt in the morning, Marcus grew irritable during breakfast. Melanie tried to reassure him, told him he was sweet, and what did one night matter, especially as there had been plenty of pleasurable moments during their relationship. But he merely scowled as he shovelled toast into his mouth, washing it down with a massive gulp of coffee. Melanie picked daintily at hers. She would have preferred muesli for breakfast but she still felt like a stranger in this house, a house that was much too large for two people. There were too many rooms, and she had only spent any time in two of them so far; the master bedroom and here in the enormous kitchen with probably more square feet than her entire Woolwich flat.

'It's not that,' he said after a long silence, and for a moment she wondered what he was talking about. 'Our lovemaking,' he elaborated. 'I'm not stupid enough to worry about our relationship just because the earth doesn't move for one night.'

'I know, Marcus. You were distracted. Your mind on other things. So, are you going to tell me what's wrong?'

79

He made a grumbling noise in the back of his throat. 'I still haven't recovered from that ghastly scene when Vanessa cornered you at the rugby club.'

Melanie shivered as her mind relived the scene in a speeded-up version. 'It was a shock. I felt terrible. Especially in front of those other people. Thank God most of the guests had gone. But there's nothing we can do about it now, is there?'

'Yes, there is. I did it the day after the funeral.'

'You did what, sweetheart?'

'I instructed one of my business associates to terminate my daughter's lease on her sandwich bar.'

Shocked, Melanie gasped. 'But don't you think – don't you think you might see things from her point of view? I expect she felt hurt, finding out her father's had a lover for quite a few years. And what with losing her mother…'

'She humiliated us. And I won't stand for it.'

'Does she know yet?'

'She received the letter yesterday. Called me up in the evening. No apologies for her behaviour. Just thinking of herself as usual.'

Melanie stretched a hand and took Marcus's in hers, gazing at him with a pleading expression. 'Oh, please, Marcus. For God's sake. I don't want to be the cause of her losing her livelihood. She'll never forgive me. I thought that given time we might—'

Marcus laughed harshly. 'Time being the healer? Don't count on it where those two are concerned. Christ! Karen can't even forgive her twin sister for that little indiscretion all those years ago. I'm sorry, but I've had it up to here with both of them.'

Melanie drew back her hand and began buttering another piece of toast. Her mouth shaped into a prissy look which further irritated her fiancé.

'And as for that little shit who's married to Karen, I shall destroy him.'

'Don't you think—'

'Don't I think what? That he can steal half a million from me and get away with it? No. I told you about him, didn't I? How he suddenly came from nowhere. Nobody really knows who he is or where he's from. He took us all in. Thought he could fool me. Yeah, and I suppose he did. Well, he's not getting away with it. There will be a reckoning.'

Melanie began to worry, fearing for her own future now. Her attentive lover was becoming obsessional and destructive. Taking revenge on strangers or business colleagues was one thing, but his own flesh and blood...

'What are you going to do about him?' she asked timidly. She suddenly felt tearful. This was all too much for her. It was a side of her lover she had never seen before. She knew he could probably be robust in his business dealings; she had heard him on the phone, the dismissive way he spoke to some business people. And now, the way he grinned, almost as if he enjoyed the anticipation of destroying his daughter's husband, was unnerving.

'First,' he said, 'I shall find out who he is. Delve into his background. I'm seeing a private investigator later this morning.'

'That's a bit dramatic, isn't it?'

'So is being rooked for half a million quid.'

Melanie nodded uncertainly, not sure how to respond to this. Aware her fiancé's attitude was seeking retribution for what he saw as an insult to his business judgement, she was taken slightly aback by his preoccupation with heaping misery on his son-in-law.

Sensing his fiancée's disapproval, Marcus said, 'I suppose you think I'm being unnecessarily harsh.'

'Not on him, maybe. From what you've told me about your son-in-law, he sounds like a conman. But I was thinking of the way it will affect your daughter. I mean, she wasn't the one who caused that scene at the rugby club.'

'No, but it's not my fault she has a knack of picking the wrong blokes. First she went out with some arsehole when she was at art college. A bearded wanker from the Middle East. Always banging on about how corrupt capitalism is – America in particular. It wouldn't surprise me if he was radicalised and is busy beheading journalists on behalf of the Jihadists.'

Melanie sniggered, and Marcus took this as encouragement to expound on his daughter's unfortunate love life.

'He was disaster number one in her life. And then she met...Oh, Christ! I've forgotten his name. He could have been one of the Mister Men. Mister Ugly. Karen was still living at home then, and whenever she brought whatever his name was round, I felt like killing him. It would have been a merciful release, not only for him but for Karen as well. Thankfully he stopped coming round after I told him to use a deodorant.'

'You didn't?'

'I bloody did. The bloke stank to high heaven. How Karen put up with it I'll never know.' Marcus looked up at the ceiling as he tried to recall. 'What was it he did? Oh yes: I think he fixed motor bikes or something. And then came the biggest disaster of all. Steve. Who was shagging her sister behind her back. I told you, didn't I? That's why they haven't spoken to each other for five years.'

'Yes, and I saw how they avoided each other at the wake.'

'Then comes number…must be number four. The tosser who thinks he can defraud me out of half a million quid. Where he came from, Christ only knows. But I'm going to make it my business to find out. There's something not quite right about him.'

'It sounds to me, Marcus, that none of them seem…well, normal.'

Marcus frowned thoughtfully. 'You're right. The others were just a bunch of tossers. But this Paul arsehole, my fucking son-in-law, is a devious little shit. And I'm going to find out which stone he's crawled from under. And if I succeed in ruining Karen's marriage, I'll be doing her an enormous favour.'

'But supposing there's nothing to discover. Suppose he's just a non-entity who's a useless businessman.'

'Oh, he is that all right. But I like to think I'm a good judge of character. And where he is concerned, I smell the proverbial. I mean, what about his parents? He's never spoken about them. And he and Karen had a quiet wedding with hardly any guests.'

'Maybe he's been brought up in a home.'

'An orphan, you mean. Yes, that had occurred to me. So now you're going to suggest I ought to be more sympathetic, yes? Charitable? Allow the guy some slack?'

Melanie shrugged, pouted, raised her coffee cup and sipped. It seemed to annoy Marcus and he made an aggressive noise in the back of his throat. Melanie put her coffee cup down and laughed.

'What's so funny?'

'You are, my darling. I don't think you know you're doing it.' He looked at her questioningly. 'That noise in your throat. Like a car revving up.'

Avoiding the criticism, he looked at his watch. 'Got some business to attend to before I see the private investigator.'

'And I'd better get back to Woolwich. I'm glad I didn't drive. Traffic'll be bad. Don't forget I'm moving in sometime in August.'

'Not for at least six weeks. And the move can't be on a weekday, especially not a Friday as I always conclude my business interests at the close of play every Friday. You know that.'

'Well, moving on a Saturday shouldn't be a problem. Better, in fact.' She let her eyes wander round the enormous kitchen, which seemed to be the focal point of the house. An enormous Aga range, copper pots and pans hanging from the ceiling, the mammoth size refrigerator and the refectory table at which she sat, all shouted luxury at her, and she wondered how he managed to keep it in pristine condition, although he had explained that a Polish woman came in to clean and tidy twice a week. French windows took up the whole of the far wall, leading to a conservatory – an add-on with natural brick down one side, opposite a wall of sliding glass doors. The conservatory contained four tall potted house plants, and comfortable-looking recliners and a white wrought iron table. Through the sliding doors was the view of a surprisingly small garden, considering how big the house was.

'Marcus?' Melanie began tentatively. 'You ever thought – now your kids are grown up and your wife has passed away – how this place might be a bit on the large side for just two of us?'

Marcus shrugged and pursed his lips. 'Maybe.'

'I mean, how many rooms has it got?'

'Twelve in total if you count the conservatory as a separate room. Leave the adjoining doors to the kitchen open and it probably becomes one room. But definitely eleven, not counting the bathrooms.'

'Bit big for two, don't you think?'

'What are you suggesting?'

'Well, this place must be worth a small fortune. We could—'

'No way, Mel. I like it here in Richmond.'

'We could stay in the district, and this house could make a small hotel. Easily.'

Marcus laughed and shook his head. 'Yeah, I suppose you mean one of those boutique hotels.'

Encouraged, Melanie added, 'And if they gave permission to convert it into a hotel, think what it could be worth.'

'Just one small obstacle, Mel. Parking. My garage has room for three cars. No more. It's metered and mainly residents' parking round the Green, and there aren't that many spaces.'

'Well, all right, maybe not a hotel. I just thought we could live somewhere nice in Richmond – maybe up on the hill – but somewhere slightly smaller.'

Marcus stood up, looked at his watch once more, and Melanie realised he was about to deliver the final word on the subject.

'I like it here on Richmond Green. Here is where it's at, Mel. It's within easy walking distance to the station, where I can catch a fast train to Waterloo in just under fifteen minutes.

'Talking of which, I need to catch one in a half hours' time. I have a meeting in the City, then I've got an appointment with this investigator to see what he can find out about that devious little prick. I'm going to enjoy shitting on him from a great height.'

As Marcus's secret lover for two years, life for Melanie had been perfect. Now she was about to find out what living together would be like, and despite her optimism for their future together, she shivered involuntarily.

Eleven

Two days after seeing the firm of private investigators, Marcus was on the train from Richmond to Waterloo when he received a phone call on his mobile from the detective agency. Bernie Flynn was the investigator dealing with his case, and the call was from his secretary.

'Hello? Marcus Bradshaw?

'Yes. That was quick. What have you got for me?'

'Can you come in and speak with Mr Flynn at your earliest convenience?'

'Can you email me the report?'

'Bernie would like to see you in person.'

'Why's that? I'm a bit busy right now.'

'Bernie specified that it was something very important. Normally he would email or send out a report such as the one you requested. But this report is of vital significance, which is why he wants a one-to-one.'

Marcus felt a ripple of excitement in his stomach. Taking a step into this cloak and dagger world gave him an instant high. And the thoughts of destroying that devious little shit would be jackpot time. Winner takes all.

'I'm just on my way to Waterloo now. I can postpone my meeting if Bernie thinks it's important.'

'He does. Extremely important, he said.'

'If Bernie's available I could be with you in just over half an hour.'

'I've checked his diary and he'll be here waiting for you.'

Marcus ended the call and sat back in his First-Class seat, a smile on his face. His imagination soared as the train rattled across the lines at Clapham Junction, and he couldn't wait to receive the intriguing information about his son-in-law.

*

The detective agency was on the top floor of a five-storey modern building just off Great Portland Street, and the reception desk faced the lift doors. As soon as they pinged open, the receptionist picked up the phone. As Marcus walked towards her, he heard her announcing his arrival.

'He's just arrived.' She looked up at him and said, 'Mr Flynn's expecting you. Go right in. It's just along the corridor to the right.'

He thanked her and turned right into the long corridor. Bernie Flynn's office was the third door along. Two days ago, when he met the private eye, Marcus expected there to be an office with all manner of gadgetry: cameras with telephoto lenses, surveillance appliances and electronic bugging devices. Instead, he was disappointed to discover just an ordinary office, minimalist, with a bookshelf displaying what looked like leather-bound law books.

As he entered. Bernie Flynn stood up to greet him and they shook hands. As soon as Marcus was seated before the private investigator's substantial desk, the private eye looked at him seriously over his half-moon glasses. He was in his mid-forties, balding, and Marcus would never have guessed what he did for a living. An accountant, maybe. Or even a schoolteacher. But never a private eye. Although, Marcus supposed, most of the information he dredged up on people was online, knowing the right places to search.

'I'm sorry I insisted on seeing you personally, Marcus. But I don't think I'd be doing my job properly if I sent you this report without offering you some advice. More than just advice. A serious warning.'

Marcus was intrigued, and his leather chair creaked as he leant forward to listen to what Flynn had to say.

'I know I sound dramatic, but the subject of this report, Paul Branson, is not who he says he is. In other words, that is not his birth name. He changed his name by deed poll following his trial for murder in North Wales ten years ago.' The investigator paused, allowing Marcus time to take in the information. 'He's been married twice. Both wives met with an accident, and he inherited their money. The first one he got away with completely, but for the second one he was charged with murder, and it went to trial about four months later.'

Marcus blew his cheeks out and shook his head. 'This is totally unexpected. I expected a few skeletons in his shitty little closet, like fraud or theft, but not murder. So what's he doing at liberty. Has he escaped or was he paroled?'

'Neither. The jury found him not guilty and accepted that it was an accident.'

'How did he kill her?'

86

'She drowned while swimming in the Menai Straits. He claimed she got cramp. He said at his trial that he did his best to rescue her but claimed he wasn't a strong enough swimmer. Apparently, a forensic scientist gave evidence saying she found nail marks on his wife's shoulders as if he had forcefully pushed her under.'

'And that wasn't enough to convict him?'

'No. He admitted grabbing his wife's shoulders but said he was doing his best to save her.'

'So, he got away with murder? And what about the first wife?'

Flynn picked up a beige folder, leant over the desk and handed it to Marcus. 'It's all in the report. The reason I wanted this meeting is because you told me he's married to one of your daughters, which is more than a bit worrying.'

Marcus opened the folder and scanned the report. 'I see he was in Scotland, and met his first wife not long after her parents died. Presumably there was some sort of inheritance?'

'We think so. We couldn't get details of just how much she was worth. All we found out is that she met with an accident less than a year after they were married.'

'She fell off a ladder while cleaning the guttering,' Marcus said as he read the report. He looked up questioningly at the investigator. 'And he was in a local pub at the time. So he had an alibi.'

Flynn shrugged and gave him a lopsided smile. 'Which wasn't far from where they lived. He could easily have knocked her off the ladder then driven to the pub. The time of her death would have been approximate – give or take a few hours. He probably claimed in his defence that it could have happened just minutes after he left to go to the pub.'

'And the police or the coroner, or whoever, just accepted it?'

'Well, unlike us, they didn't have the benefit of hindsight. Now we know he's lost wife number two *and* faced a murder charge for her unfortunate death.'

Marcus turned over a page and read more of the report. 'I see his birth name was Paul Grombard. He changed his name to Branson about seven years ago.'

Flynn snorted. 'From what you told me about him during our first meeting, the current name is self-delusional; designed to flatter him.'

'Yes, of course. It hadn't occurred to me. Branson! I should have spotted it.'

'Why would you, if you thought it was his real name?'

'The name is about as close as he got to realising his fantasies about becoming a successful entrepreneur.' Marcus stared at the report again, his eyes opening wide as more information rang bells. 'He's an only child, born and bred in Hitchin, and his parents are still alive. And you interviewed them?'

'I managed to get Mr and Mrs Grombard's telephone number. I spoke to the wife. I didn't want to worry her, so I told her I was the purser from his old school and there was going to be an old boys' reunion. But she said she couldn't help me. She said he lived abroad now – somewhere in Spain – and they occasionally received postcards from him as he had a good job that took him all over Europe. He hasn't seen them in almost twenty years. She said they would like to visit him but have never been abroad. Don't even have passports. I began to feel sorry for them.'

'I wonder if the little shit's problem stems from nature or nurture?'

'Well, I think you were right to be worried about your son-in-law. He sounds dangerous. Unhinged. And I'm sure you can appreciate why this concerns me. Now, I'm not trying to pry into your financial affairs but—'

'I'm what most people would describe as wealthy,' Marcus admitted. 'It's no great secret.'

'You told me your wife recently passed away. Does that mean your daughters would inherit your estate?'

'I see where you're coming from, Bernie. You think that after I die my son-in-law could get his hands on half my estate via my daughter?' He shook his head emphatically. 'That's not going to happen.'

'Oh? Why is that?'

'Because I'm getting married again in September. And if anything should happen to me, my wife would inherit.' Marcus spotted the fleeting look of surprise in the investigator's eyes, and decided to lie. 'I will, of course, give my daughters a generous contribution while I'm still alive. Making certain that Karen divorces her husband first. And while she has no money, and will not inherit my estate should I die—'

'After you're married,' Flynn pointed out.

'The point is: Karen is flat broke now and so is he. And until she is rid of him, I don't intend to give him a reason to kill her.'

'All the same,' said Flynn, frowning deeply, 'knowing what this man is like, she could be in danger.'

Marcus waved it aside. It was no longer his concern. He was more obsessed with getting his revenge on the son-in-law. 'I tell you what I'd like you to do, Bernie. I would like my daughter to get a copy of this report. But secretly.'

'You mean you'd like us to deliver it?'

'Exactly.'

'Do you mind if I ask you why you don't hand the report to your daughter yourself?'

'Yes, I do mind.'

The investigator saw the flash of aggression in his client's eyes, the scheming look he had seen so many times during his investigations.

'I mind very much,' Marcus added. 'I'm the client, and I would like you to carry out my instructions. What I would like you to do is keep my son-in-law under surveillance. As soon as he leaves his flat for any length of time, deliver this report to my daughter. You can tell her it came from her father and every word of it is true.'

Flynn nodded, his expression deadpan. 'Presumably you want to keep that copy. I'll get another one made up and get the ball rolling.'

'Thank you,' Marcus said as he rose. 'That'll show that arsehole how unlucky he was to tangle with the wrong person.'

Twelve

Two days after his father-in-law's meeting at the private detective agency, Paul Branson exhibited his new image, dressed now like a successful film producer. No longer the Boss or Armani suits but an expensive brown leather jacket, black jeans and brown brogues. His resilience, Karen observed, recognised no boundaries. He never endured setbacks, always pushed forward, reaching out for the success which invariably eluded him. Every decision he made was unrealistic and she began to bottle feelings of extreme anger towards him, which she concealed beneath a veneer of civilised politeness.

He came into the master bedroom where she sat at her desk, concentrating on a photoshop image she was creating for a new client. She squinted at her laptop and ignored his presence.

'I'm off for this meeting I told you about,' he announced.

'See you later then,' she replied dismissively, without taking her eyes off the screen.

Incapable of dealing with being ignored, Paul felt a niggling sensation that he was losing the battle of dominance where his wife was concerned. It was something he resented deeply, and he began to fantasise about killing her. But he knew there was no point. Nothing to be gained by it.

'Let's hope we get a buyer for the house soon,' he said. 'Then I can use some of the equity to advance this project.'

Her head swivelled in his direction. 'We need that equity for the deposit on another flat.'

Now he had her attention, the game was back to his advantage. He smiled, though his eyes were as inexpressive as glass marbles. 'Well, my sweetheart, when this film takes off, we'll be back in the fast lane again.'

Karen shook her head and smiled humourlessly, deliberately feigning amusement at his self-deception, then turned her attention back to the screen.

He had to restrain himself from dashing over and bludgeoning her with the heaviest object within reach. He controlled himself, standing immobile like a statue as he stared at her, imagining what killing her would be like. Eventually, the silence did the trick, and she looked back at him.

'Yes,' he said, 'and that twat of a father of yours will be green with envy when he sees me walking along the red carpet at a Leicester Square cinema premiere.'

'There is one true statement in that sentence, Paul.'

'Oh? What's that?'

'My father is a twat. And the cash cow has now dried up. No more help from that quarter.'

'What makes you think we'll need it when my movie takes off?'

Karen sighed deeply, looked at the screen again, and it was as if she had pushed the wrong button, because he suddenly screamed uncontrollably, 'You'd better believe it, you stupid, moronic bitch.'

She looked at him, fear in her eyes. 'I was only trying—' she began.

'I know what you were trying to do. Trying to undermine me as usual.'

'I meant I was trying to get on with this commission. This one's worth a couple of hundred.'

'Huh!' he exclaimed with a dismissive wave of his hand, then used it to point a finger at her. 'You just wait. This time next year we won't be talking hundreds but hundreds of thousands. Wait and see. Just wait and see.' He exited, shouting as he left, 'And don't bother to cook anything tonight. Or wait up for me. I'll probably be late. Very late.'

Then the door slammed. Silence.

Karen realised she'd been holding her breath throughout his tantrum and let it out slowly and tremulously, feeling tension in her back like copper wires. She rolled her shoulders several times, looked at the screen but found it difficult to concentrate now. She looked at her watch. It was almost three-thirty.

One small malt whisky couldn't hurt, could it?

She went into the kitchen, poured herself a large measure of Glenmorangie, took it back into the living room then sipped the whisky before sitting down, savouring its smooth, smoky flavour and warmth. Calmer now, able to control her emotions, she sat down and thought about Paul.

At first, she thought the film producing might be another lie or fantasy. And then, following another meeting two days ago, he came back with what he said was the final draft of the script. It had been co-written, he told her, by a real-life gangster who was heavily involved in the production. While he was out, she started to read it and got as far as page thirty-something before she got bored. The bad language in it was all that

91

she expected from a British gangster film, the plot was derivative and it contained not a single original idea. At least, as far as the first thirty-odd pages went. She thought it was a film heading straight to DVD. That was if it ever got made.

Sipping her whisky, her mind wandered as she imagined another life for herself, like a flashback in a film. If only she could rewrite and edit her past just like a film.

*

When Paul left the flat, he had already forgotten the scene with his wife. He had that ability to compartmentalise issues, and now geared himself up for big talk about making a movie. He looked forward to meeting the gangster writer again, to hear true life tales of murder and mayhem. He was so engrossed in his movie daydreams, he didn't notice the overweight man getting out of the Vauxhall Cavalier that was parked near his flat. The man waited until his quarry rounded the corner into Kingston Hill, then followed.

The man was Arthur Jones, a colleague of Bernie Flynn's, who had been given the chore of keeping Paul Branson under surveillance until he saw the opportunity of serving his wife with the report. A present from her father.

As he passed Kingston Hospital, opposite Park Road, Arthur Jones saw Branson crossing the road, and guessed he might be on his way to Norbiton railway station. He followed at a discreet distance, and saw his guess had been correct. Branson caught a train going to Waterloo.

Puffing and panting, and promising himself fewer stodgy foods and beer for a few weeks at least, the private investigator hurried back up Kingston Hill. He fetched from his Vauxhall the folder containing the report on Mrs Branson's husband, then walked up to the block of flats, pressed the intercom buzzer and waited.

'Hello?' she said. He could hear the timidity in her voice despite the crackle of the intercom.

'I have a delivery from Mr Marcus Bradshaw. A private and confidential package for Mrs Karen Branson.'

'Oh. All right. Come up to the third floor.'

The door buzzed and he let himself in to the main hall. He took the lift to the third floor and saw she was waiting for him at the open door of her flat. Frowning, her mouth open questioningly.

'Mrs Branson?' he said, holding the folder in front of him.

She closed her mouth and nodded before she spoke. 'Yes. Can I help you?'

He thought he could detect the smell of whisky on her breath, even though she stood at least half a metre away from him.

'I'm a private investigator, and your father paid us to investigate your husband's past, of which I believe you know very little. You would be surprised – perhaps horrified – at what we discovered about him. It's all here in the report.' He handed her the file. 'Please read it thoroughly, and take very good care of yourself.'

He handed her the folder. She took it tentatively, almost as if it might burn her.

'I'm not sure I understand—' she began.

'It's all there in the report.'

'Did you say this was something to do with my father?'

He nodded. 'Yes, he thought you ought to know about your husband's past.'

'Why the hell would he do that? Go to all that trouble—'

'Perhaps he was worried about you.;

'I doubt that very much.'

The investigator shuffled awkwardly and cleared his throat. He had read the report, and although he had been told to hand her the folder and leave, saying very little, he felt under the circumstances that she ought to be warned about how dangerous this Paul Branson was.

'Please. Just promise me you will read the report. It's all true. And although your husband was acquitted of murder—'

'Murder!' she broke in.

'Yes, I don't mean to alarm you, but I think it's important you read the document. We're a very reputable firm of investigators and we have reason to believe that the man – your husband – could be dangerous. Although, we were told by your father there would be no point in him harming you in the present circumstances. But you can't be too careful.' He cleared his throat noisily again. 'If you just spend time reading it, you will see what he means. Well, I must be off. I hope everything works out all right for you. Take care, Mrs Branson.'

93

Dazed, Karen thanked him, went in and shut the door. Before opening the folder, she took her whisky glass into the kitchen and poured herself another slug. She took a swallow, stood over the island work surface, and opened the folder.

She read it thoroughly three times. Then closed it and wondered about her father's motives. It was revenge, pure and simple. He hated Paul, and wanted to see him ostracised from the family. But they were no longer a family. Not now she had discovered her father had been having an affair with that young woman for several years, now planning to marry her. There was no way they could embrace the woman, allow her to be part of their family.

And what of the report? Did her father expect her to confront Paul with it?

Yes. That was what he wanted. To stir it up.

Well, little did her father realise that her only option would be to keep the report secret. She had to hide it somewhere, so Paul would never find it.

That way she could control the situation. Play the perfect wife. Obedient and willing and loving. He would never guess that she knew all about him, about his disgusting, devious past. And, of course, that man had been right. Paul had no reason to kill her. His only motive was in getting money just as soon as his schemes failed him. And now, now that her father was unlikely to help them, she had very little money.

All she could give him now was a pretence at love and affection, and be as devious as he was.

Thirteen

Marcus waved the waiter over. 'Could we have the bill, please?'

It was their favourite restaurant in Greenwich, the first one he brought her to more than two years ago. While they waited for the bill to be made up, Melanie reached across the table and squeezed his hand.

'Thank you, sweetheart. It was a lovely lunch.'

'You didn't eat very much.' He didn't want it to sound like a criticism, so added, 'No wonder you have such a stunning figure.'

Melanie accepted the compliment with a smile, and cast her eyes around the restaurant. She loved its ambience, enjoyed the attention she received and the wolfish looks she got from the young Italian waiters.

'I love this place. It was our first date. Remember?'

Marcus chuckled. 'How could I forget? The second date was in your flat.'

'And that was on the same night.'

'Well, no point in putting off till tomorrow—'

'Talking of tomorrow, will you stay at my place tonight?'

He pulled a face. 'Sorry, Mel. Tomorrow's Friday. My Fridays are sacrosanct.'

'Yes, I know,' she sighed with some reluctance. 'But if you stayed tonight, couldn't you leave first thing in the morning?'

'I need to get some work done this afternoon as well. Why d'you think I only had a half of lager with lunch?'

Melanie gave him a suggestive smile. 'I thought that might have been something to do with—'

'Being able to get it up?' he interrupted. 'I didn't disappoint last night, did I?'

The waiter brought the bill. He was a young Sicilian, dark skinned, good looking, with wavy, undulating black hair. Hearing his customer's last comment, he suppressed a smile, although his eyes sparkled for a moment as he made eye contact with Melanie, but his face remained professionally inscrutable. He slid the small silver tray with the bill onto the table and walked away.

Marcus picked up the bill, tilted his head in the direction of the departing waiter and grinned at his fiancée. 'I think if you played your cards right.'

'Don't be silly, Marcus. When I'm with you, I don't look at another man.'

'What about when you're not with me?' he joked.

'You know very well what I mean. I love you very much. You and only you.'

Yes, and you know which way your bread is buttered. The inappropriate cliché flashed through his head, and he erased it instantly.

'And I love you too, Mel,' he said as he took a wad of notes out of his pocket, peeled off two twenties and dropped them onto the plate.

Melanie always marvelled at the amount of cash he carried with him, guessed it had nothing to do with underhand business deals, but was part of his East End upbringing. It was a flashiness left over from a ducking-and-diving past, and she was attracted to this flamboyance, a stimulus that bordered on vulgarity.

As he looked at the notes on the plate, he was reminded of the invoice that arrived rapidly following the delivery of the report to his daughter. He sucked in his breath and shook his head.

'What's wrong? The bill's only half our usual one.'

'I was thinking of the bill I got from the detective agency. Seven hundred quid. Which means that little shit has cost me even more than the half million he took off me.'

Melanie laughed ironically. 'Well, much as you hate him, you can hardly hold him responsible for that extra seven hundred.'

'I know, Mel, but I feel frustrated.'

She raised her eyebrows as she looked at him enquiringly.

'I expected something to happen,' he explained. 'But a week's gone by since she received it, and nothing.'

'What did you expect to happen?'

'I don't know. But I suppose I wanted to expose him for what he is. A conniving bastard who has literally got away with murder.'

Melanie took Marcus's hand in both of hers. 'Darling, you've got to let it go. Move on. We have so much to look forward to now. And at least you've done the right thing where your daughter is concerned. You've warned her of the dangers she could face. It'll be up to her now, how she handles it.'

'You're right, Mel,' he nodded. 'I'm almost glad I lost that half million. Now it means I never need hear from that wanker again. He's out of my life completely. No ties there anymore. I can forget about him and get on with my life. Our lives.'

*

On Saturdays business was never very brisk at the sandwich bar and Vanessa usually closed around half-two. She'd been home for only an hour on the second Saturday after the funeral, feeling depressed and worrying about the future, when Alice arrived carrying a bunch of flowers.

'I thought these might cheer you up.'

Vanessa hugged her friend, then said, 'I'll put these in water. Make yourself comfortable. Coffee?'

As soon as the vase of flowers stood on the pine table, and a cafetière of coffee was made, Alice looked across the table at her friend, a concerned frown on her face. Vanessa looked ill, her face pallid and puffy, and there were dark streaks like tyre marks under her eyes.

'Have you not been sleeping?' Alice asked.

'Hardly at all. Been worrying. My brain, and all the hatred in it, won't let me sleep. Maybe two or three hours a night. Not much more.'

Alice cleared her throat gently. She had already heard the full story of the grim funeral, and of the catastrophic uproar at the wake, and knew Vanessa wanted to talk it through again, as if it were some sort of unbelievable story that had happened to someone else. But, if Alice had to admit it, the repetition of the incident was becoming tedious, and much as she tried to listen and empathise, her sympathy began to dwindle.

'I still can't believe my father gave the word to have me evicted,' Vanessa said. 'You would think, wouldn't you, that he would have made allowances for my behaviour at the funeral.'

Alice gave a slight nod. 'His own behaviour was appalling – bringing his mistress to his wife's funeral. That was despicable.'

'I hated him then. I've never hated anyone so much in all my life.'

These sorts of conversations since the funeral incident had gone round in circles, so Alice decided to probe a little deeper. Find out what her friend thought about the inheritance situation.

'I hope you don't mind me asking,' she began, 'but presumably if he marries this woman—'

'Not if, but when!' Vanessa interrupted.

'OK. When they get married. Presumably, when your father eventually dies, she stands to inherit everything, and you and your sister will get nothing. That seems grossly unfair. And it seems as if he's letting his cock rule his heart.'

Vanessa laughed bitterly. 'Heart! Don't make me laugh. That man has no heart. He thinks of only himself. Ever since the funeral, I've hated him so much, I've wished him dead many times.'

'And if he did die – meet with an accident – you and your sister would stand to gain. Everything would come to you two.'

'What are you saying?'

'Well, that's it really. All I'm saying is, I don't suppose anyone could blame you if you were pleased if he has a major heart attack or an accident before September.'

Vanessa looked uncomfortable and avoided eye contact with Alice. 'I suppose,' she said, 'I might say things like how I wish he was dead, and how much I hate him – that sort of thing – but when it boils down to it, he is my father, when all's said and done.'

'So, it's really just words – you wishing him dead. Getting it off your chest.'

'Yes, of course. Bastard he may be, but he's still my father.'

'I'm glad to hear it. But another thought has occurred to me. This is a hypothetical one. Suppose – just suppose – he's already made a new will, leaving everything to this woman, and he dies before he marries her.'

'I would think we could dispute that in court. But, as you say, this is all hypothetical, and eventually I'm going to have to sort myself out. Move on, find something else I can do. I've got just over six weeks before the sandwich bar closes, and then who knows.'

'And is there really no way of mending this rift?'

'I doubt it. He knows I'm never going to accept this woman.'

'And, given time, can't you just accept the way things are? Put it down to your father's stupidity? A late mid-life crisis.'

'Maybe. I don't know. I don't care anymore.'

Vanessa shrugged, and Alice got the impression her friend wanted the subject to end, which was unusual considering the way Vanessa's family problems had dominated every conversation up until now. But Alice was relieved. At least they could revert to other topics of conversation, even though she realised that what they had in the early part of their friendship was lost. The humour that bound them together was gone. And now that the conversation no longer revolved around Vanessa's problems, the small-talk became stilted and awkward.

Alice glanced at her watch. 'I think I'd better make a move. I'm off out with Peter tonight. To the theatre.'

Peter was a new man in her life, and she was disappointed when Vanessa merely nodded without asking for any information, however trivial. Alice became aware – and not for the first time – that every conversation had to revolve around her friend. But then she felt guilty for having this conclusive opinion. After all, Vanessa was the one with major family problems. Still, she was glad she had an excuse to get out of the sapping atmosphere of the flat.

She was at the front door when Vanessa rushed forward with a letter in her hand. 'You couldn't post this for me, could you? Only I don't think I want to go out today. I've got things to do.'

'What are you up to that's so important?' Alice said as she took the letter, and couldn't help but notice the name and address on the front.

Vanessa shrugged. 'Oh, nothing important. Just need to get my head round things.'

'I see you're writing to your sister. That's her name, isn't it? Karen Branson.'

'Yes. It's another attempt to resolve things between us.'

Alice smiled. 'I'll make sure this goes from the main post office at Charing Cross this evening. That means your sister will get it on Monday. I hope things work out for you this time.'

'So do I,' Vanessa said, blowing her friend a goodbye kiss as she closed the front door. She leaned back on it, blew out a relieved sigh and repeated, 'So do I.'

*

As they sat at the table on Monday morning enjoying a breakfast of fruit, yoghurt and coffee, Karen noticed Paul was dressed in his trendy Aladdin Sane T-shirt, with his leather jacket draped over the back of his chair. The new image.

'What's on the agenda today?' Karen asked.

Paul stopped stirring blackcurrants into his plain yoghurt and looked at her through narrowing eyes, as though she had challenged him about something.

'What do you mean?'

'I just wondered what you're up to, that's all.'

'A meeting with the writer and director of the film. I hope that meets with your approval.'

'Of course it does. Why wouldn't it?'

'Last week you were against everything to do with this project. That's why.'

'Well, I've had time to think about it, and I think it's a good idea in principle.'

Paul frowned deeply, confused by his wife's sudden volte-face. 'So why now have you decided to compromise where the film is concerned.'

'Who said anything about compromise?' she replied, staring at him with what she hoped was an expression of utter sincerity. 'I'm with you one hundred per cent on this. I think, having read the script thoroughly, it could be a winner.'

'And what about the equity on the house if I decide to use some of the money to forward the project?'

'Well, I think you're right. If the film takes off, we stand to gain a great deal more than any of our other prospects.'

'What other prospects?'

'Exactly. My father won't have anything to do with us now. Not financially, anyway. And when he marries in September, then his new wife stands to inherit his estate. Which is considerable. And the house in Richmond is worth around six or seven million. Maybe more. And I or my sister wouldn't get a penny.'

'Miserable bastard,' he grumbled.

'So, you see, our best bet is to make this film work. And now, thinking of you, my husband, becoming a film producer…well, it's exciting. Very exciting.'

She wondered if she had gone too far, because she saw the narrowing of the eyes again as he said, 'And you don't mind that the co-writer on this film was the notorious Terry Lennox, the east End gangster who—'

'Of course I don't,' she interrupted with a show of enthusiasm. 'That's what will give it authenticity. He clearly knows what he's talking about.'

But she could tell from the way Paul looked at her that he was still suspicious. She saw his mind analysing and sifting through all that she had said, causing a gear-shift in his brain that confused him.

'And you don't—' he began, but was interrupted by the sound of the letter box and letters dropping onto the mat.

Wondering what he was about to say, but relieved by the interruption, she was glad of the excuse to rise from the table.

'It's OK,' he said. 'I'll get it.'

Knowing he liked to collect the post, and suspected it was because he could conceal any creditors' letters, she sat down again and waited. Presently he returned carrying three envelopes.

'Two junk mail,' he said. 'And one for you. Handwritten.' He handed her the envelope, then stood over her, inquisitive and demanding. 'Who's it from?'

'It's from my sister. I recognise her handwriting.'

'She can't have sent you a birthday or Christmas card for over five years. How come you know it's from her.'

'No one's handwriting changes over the years. Perhaps it deteriorates a bit as we use word processors more and more, but—'

'Well, aren't you going to open it? he demanded impatiently.

She slit open the envelope and pulled out the one sheet of lined A4 paper. 'It's from Vanessa,' she said, as her eyes scanned the page.

'What does she say, sweetheart?'

'I'll read it to you, if you like. "Dear Karen, I know this letter out of the blue will come as a surprise – or perhaps a shock. But I still am truly sorry about all that's happened between us. Please can we be friends once more. I know Mummy wanted us to be friends again, and I know she passed away before that happened, but please for the sake of her memory, let us be a family once more, especially as we no longer seem to be our father's daughters. Only our dear mother's, God rest her soul.

'"Please come and see me. Perhaps you could come to the A Star Sandwich Bar which I run. It's near Turnham Green station, and is between a bookmaker and dry cleaners. It's easy to find. Please visit me, and we can at least talk it over. Yours hopefully, your loving sister, Vanessa".'

Karen's face was contorted with rage as she screwed the letter up and threw it on the table. 'Loving sister!' she sneered. 'Two-faced bitch.'

'Christ!' Paul exclaimed. 'You really hate her, don't you?'

'Yes, I still hate her. And my father.' Getting up from the table, she began to clear the breakfast things.

Paul grabbed his leather jacket from the chair and slipped it on. 'I'd better get going,' he said.

Karen was about to leave the room, carrying two bowls and coffee mugs, and happened to turn back to say goodbye to her husband when she saw him reading Vanessa's letter which he had unfolded and smoothed out.

'What are you doing?' she asked.

'Oh, I dunno. Just having a read of her letter again. She has nice handwriting.'

Smiling, Karen took some of the crockery to the kitchen and loaded it in the dishwasher. She thought she was over the hurdle now, certain she had convinced Paul on how he had her wholehearted support. The perfect, devoted little wifey. Now she felt safe, because he had absolutely no reason to harm her. None at all. And although she knew just how devious he could be, she could be twice as devious, and felt she had the upper hand now that she had read that report.

Fourteen

She had met Karen's husband only once but Vanessa recognised him straightaway when he walked into the sandwich bar. Dressed now as the thrusting business man in his Boss suit and lemon-yellow silk tie, he offered her his most seraphic smile as he approached the counter.

'I don't suppose you remember me,' he said, the angelic smile becoming cocksure as he noticed the way her eyes lit up as they met his.

She clicked her fingers and pointed at him. 'Remind me.'

He knew she was teasing him, and liked her for it. 'Your twin's husband. Paul.'

'Ah, yes. But what are you doing here?'

'I was in the district touting for business and I remembered the name of your café from the letter you wrote to your sister yesterday.'

'Right. And how did my sister respond to my plea of reconciliation?'

He shook his head and pursed his lips. 'Badly, I'm afraid. Called you a bitch and screwed up the letter. Somehow I don't think your differences will be resolved very soon.'

'They certainly won't be if she finds out you've been to see me.'

He grinned cockily. 'I won't tell her if you don't.'

'Now look!' she said, slapping an assertive hand onto the counter. 'You coming in here can only make things worse between us. You know the reason for our falling out, I take it.'

'Sure. It was because of the affair you had with her fiancé. Was it worth it?'

'No. And you stirring things up by coming in here—'

'Whoa!' he exclaimed, raising a hand to silence her. 'You are family, after all. My sister-in-law. I just happened to be passing, thought I'd get to know you, and have a quick cup of coffee. That's all.'

'I was just closing – as you can see.'

'Well, no coffee then. Maybe something stronger. There must be a pub nearby.'

'There's one just round the corner on the main road. Enjoy your drink.'

'I don't like drinking on my own, Vanessa. Why not join me?'

She sighed, turned her back on him, and removed her apron. 'I think that's a terrible idea. Suppose we bumped into someone who knows Karen.' She bent down and picked up her handbag from behind the counter; when she straightened up and looked at her brother-in-law, she saw him grinning confidently.

'And is that the only reason you won't come and have a drink with me? On the off-chance someone who knows Karen might see you?'

Vanessa hesitated. 'Well, I—'

'I mean, things can't get any worse between you and her. She hasn't spoken to you for five years, so even if she found out about us having a drink together – and I doubt that she would – what the hell does it matter?'

Vanessa locked eyes with him and thought she saw something sinister buried deep inside his head. And she knew if she went for a drink with this man there would be no turning back. It was decision time. And it was her call.

Simple. Like the toss of a coin.

'OK,' she said. 'I'll come for a drink.'

*

They managed to find a table in a quiet corner of the pub. Vanessa looked furtive, glancing around the vast bar like a fugitive, hoping she wouldn't bump into Alice. If she had to introduce Paul as her brother-in-law she knew it would send her friend into a spiral of disapproval. Although Vanessa knew she was worrying unnecessarily, because Alice invariably rang first and rarely turned up unexpectedly.

Noticing her discomfort, Paul smiled and told her to relax. She was about to take a sip of her white wine when Paul raised his red wine and clinked glasses with her. 'Cheers! So, tell me, what made you decide to have a drink with me?'

She shrugged. 'I don't know. I suppose it's because – since Mummy died – I don't care about anyone in my family. Although, that's not strictly true, I love my aunty and nephews, but they live in New York. And my Aunty Christine has made it clear that neither Karen or I will be welcome there until we iron out our differences.'

'And that's not likely to happen soon. Karen told me about how you freaked out after the funeral.'

'I still can't believe how that man who calls himself my father—'
Unable to continue at the memory of her father's audacious behaviour and
treachery, she stopped herself from swearing loudly as she pictured his
hateful face. She knocked back half of her large glass of wine instead.

Paul studied her carefully before changing the subject. 'How's the
sandwich bar doing? Business good, is it?'

'It was OK. But now I've lost it.'

'What d'you mean, you've lost it?'

She told him about the letter arriving two days after the funeral, giving
two months' notice to quit. He noticed her body language when she spoke
of her father, the clenched fists and the way her jaw jutted forwards
angrily, like a vicious animal ready to tear the guts out of its prey.
Through tightened lips, barely opening her mouth, she told him how much
she hated her father for what he was doing to her. At the end of her
diatribe, she looked him in the eye and asked, 'And what about you,
Paul?'

'I'm not with you.'

'Well, I heard about him standing as guarantor for your business which
has gone bust. And he reckons you owe him half a million quid.'

'Huh! He can reckon all he likes. He knew the risks. I owe him sod all.'

'No, but he won't see it like that. He's deranged and demented. It's a
serious game to my father, a horrible game which he seems intent on
winning.'

'Yes, apparently, he told Karen that he'll be gunning for me.'

'That's true. I was there when he said it.'

Paul leant back in his seat, a smug expression on his face. 'That was just
talk. What can he do to me?'

'You'd be surprised. He seems to be out for revenge. And he can get at
you through Karen.'

'Yeah, but my business has gone kaput, the house is on the market, and
we are flat broke. So, there's nothing else he can do, is there? And my
next project when it comes off will shake him up. He'll be livid, while I
will be giving him the finger.'

'Why? What's your next project?'

He leaned forward and, elbow resting on the table, waved a limp-wristed
hand nonchalantly. 'I know it sounds a bit grand. But you are looking at a
film producer.'

Vanessa's eyes widened. 'Really?'

'Yes. Really. A low budget gangster movie. Three million.'

'Where will you find that sort of money?'

'Investors, of course. You don't finance a film with your own money. But I need money for the schmoozing of investors and the day-to-day running expenses, which can be considerable.'

Vanessa smiled knowingly. 'So you thought you'd woo the sister – history repeating itself – knowing I have my own business, and could help you finance your dreams.'

'No, of course not. I just happened to be in the area—'

'Well, you're out of luck, because in six weeks' time I will also be flat broke and out of a job. And that fucking scrubber will be his new family, which he will no doubt spoil rotten. Christ! I hate him. How is it possible to hate the man who made you? Did he love my mother? I doubt it. She was his trophy wife, and the moment Karen and I were conceived was probably just another of his many shags. He may be my father in a legal sense, but I feel he's no more my father than any man who cold-heartedly screws a woman then pisses off.'

'D'you think he's made a new will favouring his fiancée?'

'He might have done, but I doubt it. He's not going to think anything will happen to him between now and September.'

A fraction of a cruel smile pulled at the corners of Paul's mouth as he said, 'But suppose something did happen to him.'

'An accident, you mean? How likely is that?'

His smile became distinctly visible now. 'Accidents can sometimes be made to happen.'

'What are you suggesting?'

'Just doing a bit of wishful thinking. I mean, if something were to happen to your father before he marries this woman, you and your sister will get an equal share of his estate. As Karen's husband, even if we were to split up, I would be entitled to a half share of what she inherits. Not that it would come to that as Karen's been quite supportive recently, so I get to make my gangster movie. And you, Vanessa, can live your dreams and ambitions, whatever they are.'

'But, like you said, this is just wishful thinking.'

'It doesn't have to be.'

Vanessa's mouth opened in shock. 'He's my father for God's sake.'

'But you said yourself it's only in a legal sense. You don't love him or like him. You hate him, don't you?'

106

'Yes,' she hissed. 'Like I've never hated anyone before. Whenever I picture his face, I want to smash it with a hammer.'

He leant forward, looking at her intently, and lowered his voice. 'If I could find a man who knows a man who could nick a car and do a hit and run, would you care?'

There was a long pause while she thought about it. 'Yes, I would care very much.'

Disappointed, he leant back again and sighed.

'But for very different reasons,' she added. 'Involve too many people in a plan and it's bound to fail.'

It took a while to sink in, but when it did, he grinned broadly. 'So, what do you suggest?'

She looked over her shoulder quickly before speaking. 'I suggest we go back to my place and discuss it in private.'

Fifteen

As soon as they entered Vanessa's flat, Paul looked round, his eyes photographing everything. He reminded her of one of those detectives in a television drama, inquisitive and looking for clues. She studied his reaction, but his expression was hard to read. Approval of her taste in furniture or disapproval? It was hard to tell.

'Nice place you've got here,' he said. 'And I quite like Ikea furniture.' Spotting an affronted expression in the downward sweep of her mouth, he added, 'No, really. I do. And it's good that you've got your own separate entrance to the flat. I suppose it's more of a maisonette, with the steps on the outside of the building leading up to your place. Who lives in the one downstairs?'

'An elderly couple. Both in their eighties.'

D'you have much to do with them?'

'I hardly ever see them. Now and again. Mostly the old boy. She's got Parkinson's and hardly ever goes out?'

'What about playing music? I mean you, of course. D'you have to keep the noise down?'

She pursed her lips before answering. 'I've never really thought about it. I play the TV and music at a reasonable level, I suppose. I don't have to creep around, if that's what you mean. I wouldn't think my neighbours' hearing is very good, considering their age.'

He seemed satisfied with her answers and she got the impression he was initiating the early stages of a plot.

'I've got a bottle of white wine in the fridge,' she announced.

'A glass of wine will help.'

She looked at him questioningly. 'Help?'

'Yes. To stimulate our ideas at this early stage.'

While Paul sat the pine table, and Vanessa fetched the wine, he thought about his prospects. If Karen's sister was serious about having her father killed, then he stood to gain a half share in a fortune. And there would be no need to kill Karen. A simple divorce would leave him with quite a few million. That was if he and Vanessa could pull off the perfect crime, and he had no reason to doubt that they could. It would just take a great deal of study and application, anticipating all the things that could go wrong. Details, that was what counted, where not even the smallest detail was overlooked.

Vanessa returned from the kitchen with a bottle of Pinot Grigio and poured out two large glasses. By the serious expression on her face, he was sensitive enough to adapt to the gravity of the situation, and feigned a sombre demeanour. Unsmiling, he accepted the glass and refrained from toasting her or saying anything. He would leave it to her to make the first move.

As he waited, watching while she sipped her wine, he fancied he could hear a clock ticking, then realised it was in his head. There was no clock in the room.

'I suppose you think I'm callous,' she began.

He shook his head and waited for her to continue. This was a delicate manoeuvre, plotting to kill her father. It would take a great deal of understanding and Machiavellian manipulation.

'But I want that man dead. I need closure. And the only way I will get that, and can come to terms with the way he's behaved throughout my mother's illness, will be if he dies. I suppose you think I want him dead because of the money.'

He noticed the way she objectified her father now, referring to him in general terms. Wanting 'that man dead'. He remained silent, shook his head, and let her continue.

'I want to do some good with the inheritance,' she said, staring into the distance. 'Do something ethical with the money he's made from other people's misery. All his life he's been ruthless, making money purely for his own pleasure. And the only way I can do this is by putting him out of his misery.'

He coughed delicately. 'It will take a good deal of planning.'

'And we need to move quickly.'

'Before September, when they get married,' he agreed.

'No, even sooner. It's the last week in May, and I remember him saying after the funeral that he and that fucking little tart are off on a week's holiday the second week in June. And she also plans to move in with him. I think, from what he said, it would be about six weeks from the funeral.'

'Which means we are looking towards the beginning of August. A month away.'

She sipped her wine thoughtfully and stared at him, scrutinising his personable face for any hint of viciousness. 'Have you ever killed anyone?'

He frowned. 'No, of course not. Why would you ask me that?'

'Because I want to know if you're cold-blooded enough to go through with it.'

'Unlike you, hating your father and feeling the need to use his money to do good works, I need that money to make this picture. I could then finance it myself. Apart from which, your father is out to get me. I know he's planning some sort of revenge. Was it my fault the travel agency went bust? I hate the bastard, and I would have no regrets about squashing him like a cockroach. So, believe me, I can do it. Without losing any sleep.'

'OK. Now we've agreed to do it, we need to work out how.'

'I agree with you, Vanessa, up to a point. The less people we involve the better. But it can't be an accident, and there is no point in even trying to make it look like an accident.'

'Why not?'

'Well, he wants nothing to do with me, you or Karen. So, there's no way we can get anywhere near him to make his death look accidental.'

'When you say 'we', I think the only way this will work is if you do the crime, and I become your perfect alibi.'

A glint came into his eye. 'I think I see where you're coming from. Because you had an affair with Karen's fiancé five years ago, it might be a case of history repeating itself. You and I become lovers. And on the night your father meets his maker, I'm here with you. All night.'

'That could work.'

'And,' he said slowly, a lascivious smile on his face, 'that's the sort of alibi I'm going to enjoy.'

'The affair we are allegedly going to have will be on paper.'

'How d'you mean?'

'I mean, we're not really going to have an affair. If the police question us, we will reluctantly confess to being lovers. With great reluctance. These will be important details we need to work out.'

He grinned. 'You have just echoed some of my earlier thoughts. The importance of details. And one of those important details might be for us to become lovers. For the sake of authenticity.'

'I'm sorry, Paul. No way.'

'Why not?'

'Because what we are about to do is a serious business, and the only way I want to get involved with you is through this…this…'

'Murder,' he said, and saw her wince. 'We can't beat about the bush, using polite euphemisms to describe the plot to murder your father. And if I do the actual murder, the fact that you are a conspirator makes you just as guilty in the eyes of the law. You still want to go through with it?'

Although the temperature was almost twenty centigrade outside, Vanessa shivered. Then her mouth set tight in a determined expression and she grabbed the wine bottle and topped up their glasses.

'I hate him. And I know he hates us. Nothing has changed. I'm prepared to go through with it.'

Paul nodded. 'Good. Now what we have to work out is the when and the how.'

'If he goes on holiday for a week, it should be done on the first Friday after he returns.'

'Why then?

'He always keeps Friday free to finish off any remaining business until the following week. When I was young, if we made any noise on a Friday afternoon or evening, he'd go berserk. Mummy would invariably take us out somewhere – often to the pictures when we were a bit older. Now on a Friday, he'll have that house to himself and won't want to be disturbed.'

'Does he have any enemies?'

'Dozens, I should think. People he's done the dirty on in business.'

'So, there could be many people who have a motive to kill him. And if you are my alibi—'

'It could work. So long as you leave no traces at the house.'

'But how the hell would I get into the house? He's hardly going to invite me in.'

Vanessa sipped her wine, savouring the drama of the situation. She felt excited now. This was unreal, something happening in a dream. She was about to cross the line and it was like leaving behind everything in her past and starting afresh.

After a brief pause, she put down her glass and said, 'Getting into the house is the easy part. I've got a key to the front door. Karen has too. We always let ourselves in when we went to visit Mummy. He wouldn't have dared change the locks while she was still alive.'

'But I can't just use your key and let myself in.'

111

'Why not? If the police question me about the key, I'll deny having it still – say that my father asked for it back after Mummy passed away and because I no longer live there.'

'But this is stupid. I can't just walk in using the front door key.'

'But don't you see,' Vanessa emphasised, shaking her head, 'they won't know someone has let themselves in. It could be a visitor, one of his business enemies, come to plead with him, talk things over. Then his rival loses his temper and kills him. That would be much more convincing than a break-in and burglary gone wrong.'

Paul looked out of the window, thinking deeply. 'It could just work. How will I do it, though?' He looked back at Vanessa. 'Admittedly your father is older than me, but something tells me he's able to take care of himself. He looks quite strong. The only way to do this will be with a gun.'

'Where can you get a gun from?'

'There are ways.'

Vanessa bristled. 'No, come on. We can't have secrets from each other. I have to know exactly what's going on.'

'One of the co-writers of my film is an East End villain—'

'But he'll want to know why you want the gun,' she protested. 'And then when he hears of the shooting, he'll know exactly who was responsible.'

Paul smiled complacently. 'I'm his producer. And he's desperate to get this film made. He's not getting any younger, and if I tell him that getting me a gun means I'll be able to completely finance the film myself, believe me, he won't say a word to anyone.'

'But he's a villain. Can he be trusted?'

'Have you heard of Terry Lennox? His trial lasted almost four weeks, for the murder of three drug dealers in their Range Rover. They were found in their blood-splattered vehicle in a field by the Dartford crossing. He had excellent legal representation and was acquitted. And, although he ran a huge firm of gangsters, he's never been inside for so much as being drunk and disorderly.'

'When was this?'

'In the seventies.'

'It was before my time. I was born in 1989.'

'Well I was still in nappies when this happened. I'm just trying to point out that Terry won't want to risk a prison sentence this late in his life for supplying someone with a firearm. I can guarantee he'll keep quiet about it. *And* he wants to see the film made.'

'OK. Let us suppose he can get you a gun—'

'If anyone can, Terry can. Believe me.'

'All right. So, it's a Friday evening on the last week in June, and it'll still be light when you turn up there at about nine p.m.'

Paul raised his hand. 'Wait! Why can't it be a bit later, when it's at least getting dark?'

'Because where Fridays are concerned he's pretty much a creature of habit. He may work until about ten, and then pop out to the Cricketers or the White Swan for a few pints.'

'What happens if he knocks off much earlier?'

'Go in and wait for him. He'll be back after eleven. Then you'll still be in time to catch an Underground train at Richmond station. We can look up the times of the last trains. But I don't think it'll be a problem if you arrive at nine. I think he'll still be there?'

'Let me get this straight. You're suggesting I do the job, then walk to Richmond station?'

'Why not? You can change your appearance. Wear trainers, track suit bottoms and a baseball cap. When you leave the house, turn into Old Palace Lane which will take you down to the river. That's where you can get rid of the gun. Chuck it in the river. You'll have to make sure you're not seen – by someone walking their dog or walking home from the pub. And you can get rid of the key in the river, as well. Then after you pass the White Cross Hotel, which is a large pub just before Richmond Bridge, turn into Water Lane which will bring you out into George Street. Then it's just a short walk to the station.'

'Christ! Anyone'd think you'd done this sort of thing before,' he said admiringly.

'It's just that I know the area so well. I grew up there, remember.'

'So, I just jump on a train to – where's your nearest station?'

'Gunnersbury.' She paused while she thought about it, then shook her head. 'Don't get off at Gunnersbury. Go another three stops and get off at Ravenscourt Park. We'll find a side street nearby – somewhere where there is no CCTV, and I'll pick you up there. You can send me a text when you get on the train at Richmond, and if I leave straightaway, I should be there waiting for you.'

'Then I come back here for a night of passion.'

She eyed him coldly. 'You can bed down on the sofa. Let's get this straight from the start. Our affair is purely an invention. Your perfect alibi.'

'Fair enough. But you can't blame me for trying. You're a very attractive woman.'

She ignored the compliment, and continued refining the plan. 'We'll need to buy two disposable mobile phones and use them just once. And you drive I take it?'

He nodded. 'BMW.'

'Park it round the corner from here. There's a street that runs parallel to this one, and there's always plenty of spaces at this end, where there's a scout hut. I'll leave my car outside here, so I can drive straight to Ravenscourt Park to meet you.'

'It could be around half-ten by the time I get back. You never know. What if someone coming home sees you leaving at that time?'

'I'll call in at the first off-licence in Chiswick High Road, buy some wine – as if we've run out – and make sure I get a receipt for it. That should explain my going out at that time. But I don't think it will be necessary. It's just good to have every eventuality covered.'

Paul grinned confidently. 'Christ! These details will give us a watertight plan. You seem to have thought of everything.'

'Well, working this out as we go along is surprisingly easy, you have to admit.'

'I'm impressed. What else do we need to know?' He clicked his fingers. 'Of course. Security at the house. Any burglar alarms or CCTV?'

'There is a camera that covers the front entrance, but when he's home on a Friday it's not switched on. Just in case it is, I can tell you exactly where the monitor is in his study on the first floor. If he's in, the burglar alarm will be switched off. In the unlikely event of his going out early to the pub, the alarm will give you a minute to type in the code. You'll find it in the kitchen, in a small box on the wall just behind the door. You can commit the code to memory. It's only four digits and a hashtag. There's an easy way to remember it. Think of the Battle of Hastings and go forward a hundred and one years.'

'Eleven sixty-seven?'

'Spot on. And don't forget the hashtag afterwards. Not that I think you'll need to disable the alarm. I think he'll be home. Working. If he's only just got back from a week's holiday, he'll have a great deal to catch up on.'

114

Paul rubbed his forehead worriedly. 'But that's what bothers me. What we've talked about up to now is the idea that someone from his past, someone he knows – a business rival he may have cheated – arrives at the front door, is invited inside and then kills him. If someone came in and disabled the alarm, the police will know that it's someone connected to his family. How else would they know the code?'

'I think you're worrying unduly. I think he'll still be at home then.'

'But what if he's not?'

'No one will know that he didn't go out to the pub and forgot to switch the alarm on. It won't be switched on, that's all. And even if he's out, and doesn't come back from the pub until well past eleven, it doesn't matter. The mysterious visitor could have arrived any time.'

'But if your old man's not home, wouldn't it be safer to postpone it until the following Friday?'

Vanessa shook her head fervently. 'No. Definitely not. I think it's got to be as soon as possible.'

'I don't understand. Why are you in such a hurry?'

'Because we can't risk leaving it until she moves in with him. That would complicate things.'

'I would have thought—'

'That I'd want her dead as well. Is that what you were going to say?'

'It had occurred to me.'

'She's only a few years older than me. I don't want her death on my conscience.'

'OK,' he agreed. 'We do this in a couple of weeks' time. Can you get me a spare key?'

'No. Make sure the one I give you is the only one you use and then get rid of it with the gun.'

'I meant a key to your flat.'

'Why d'you want a key to my flat?'

'I'm supposed to be your lover, coming round here regularly.'

She paused as she considered his suggestion, then said, 'I don't think that's a good idea. I think it's far better that we behave as if we've only just started an affair. If we're interviewed by the police, any expressions of guilt on our faces they will interpret as the recent adultery, for which you will, of course, feel a great deal of shame and remorse for having screwed your wife's sister. It'll be far more believable if we play it as a spur of the moment impulsive act. We don't have time to establish this alibi as a long-

115

term affair. I just think it might look suspicious if you're searched, and they find you with a key to my flat. And when we're interviewed by the police, it will be separately, so we need to be absolutely clear how this impulsive affair happened.'

'And I ought to be the one to shoulder most of the blame,' he elaborated. 'When you wrote to your sister, hoping she might forgive you, I memorised your sandwich bar address and came looking for you.'

She looked at him knowingly. 'Which is exactly what has happened.'

'And even if Karen has trashed that letter,' he said, 'she will still be able to confirm receiving it. But there are many other details we need to cover.'

'Such as?'

'You talked about me dressing up disguised as a chav. If someone in the area notices me leaving here on the Friday night, it could go horribly wrong. Just one mistake like that, and the plan is scuppered.'

She nodded gently as she thought about it. 'You'll need to leave here quite early, as people are leaving work on a Friday evening. You can dress normally, into something nondescript, and have the change of clothes in a backpack.'

'Along with the gun,' he added.

'Yes, along with the gun. And I can drop you somewhere busy – somewhere like Hammersmith. The pubs'll be jam-packed on a Friday evening. Sit in a corner, reading a book and minding your own business. No one will notice you. Then, when it's almost time to go to Richmond, go into the loo and change into the other gear. And when you get the train to Richmond, don't forget to pay cash for your ticket.'

Annoyed, Paul replied, 'You think I'm stupid or something?'

'Sorry. Yes, I suppose that is a bit obvious. I just wanted to make sure we've covered everything. And, don't forget, buy a cheap pay-as-you-go from a supermarket, and I'll do the same. We'll exchange numbers, and we won't use them until that one vital phone call when I come to pick you up. Then we can get rid of them.'

'And I'll need to get rid of the clothes I was wearing.'

She waved the suggestion aside, as if it was the least of their problems. 'Oh, I'll see to that.'

'Yes, but how?'

'I'll still do the sandwich bar on Saturday morning. I can get rid of them then. And you can stay here and wait for me to get back.'

He clicked his fingers again. 'Just had an idea. If you come back Saturday afternoon, and as I leave to go home, we could have a bloody great row outside.'

'To draw attention to the fact that you stayed with me. Yeah, why not?'

'Just one more thing,' he said. 'I'll need money to buy the gun. I've no idea of the going rate for an illegal weapon.'

'Don't worry. We'll manage.'

'I imagine it could be expensive.'

'I said, we'll manage.'

'I was sort of thinking of a wasted expense.'

Disconcerted, she frowned and shook her head. 'Why would it be wasted?'

'Let's get this clear: we are planning to murder your father. Between now and the next couple of weeks, you might change your mind. And if we go to the expense of buying—'

Vanessa slammed a fist onto the table. 'I'm committed. I've made up my mind.'

She felt a prickle of tears but controlled herself, her jaw set tight with determination. It was a roller coaster ride as her brain reeled with images of her father, lying naked with that bitch; images she had never imagined with her mother. Her mother was on a pedestal, someone to be worshipped and admired, and now she was gone forever, leaving Vanessa with what she despised the most, the heartless and acerbic taste of her father, and the wanton picture of him cavorting with the slut who stood to inherit his estate when he was gone. It was so unfair. Like being thrown out, discarded like rubbish, as though the past didn't matter. How could he do that to her and her sister? The only way she could reclaim her life, and the beautiful memories of her mother, was if her father vanished. Almost as if he had never existed. No longer a part of her past and fond memories. It was like washing the dirt away.

'There is no way back now,' she told Paul. 'None at all.'

He smiled and nodded, and seemed to understand, for which she was grateful.

Sixteen

Just before the cab pulled up outside the preview cinema in Wardour Street, Marcus asked Melanie, 'Remind me: what are we going to see again?'

Irritation crept into her tone. 'How many more times do I have to tell you? It's called *Killer Ghoul*. It's a horror film.'

Laughing, he said, 'Not a romantic comedy then.'

'Hardly, darling. And romantic comedies are called romcoms.'

Marcus slid open the window, handed the driver a twenty and told him to keep the change. Almost a five-pound tip, Melanie calculated as they walked into the reception area of the viewing room. When it came to business, her fiancé could be ruthlessly tight-fisted, yet when he was socialising he thrust his wealth down everyone's throat with ostentatious displays of generosity.

The reception, not a particularly large area, was crammed with people, and at a long table two young women served red or white wine, bottles of Beck's lager, orange juice or mineral water. A young actor spotted Melanie, excused himself from a group, and came forward to greet her. Marcus noticed how the young man – probably in his late-twenties – fancied her.

'Ray!' Melanie said loudly, and so excitedly it succeeded in annoying Marcus.

Before she could introduce Marcus to the young man, he said, 'I'll go and get us a drink,' and elbowed his way towards the drinks table. When he came back with two glasses of wine, another three men had joined his fiancée. There was a slightly awkward hiatus as he joined the group, and suddenly he felt that Melanie was embarrassed by his presence, and might have preferred to come to the screening by herself. Then he remembered how much she insisted on him attending the event, and his self-doubts vanished. Marcus never felt insecure for more than a passing whisper of time.

Following a mercifully short conversation, where Marcus learnt that the young man was the star of *Killer Ghoul*, and was a regular actor in *Emmerdale*, a soap Marcus confessed he had never seen, they were asked to take their seats for the start of the film, and were told they could bring their drinks into the small 150-seat cinema.

As soon as the film began, with its deliberate out-of-focus shots and blaring music, right away he knew he was going to hate it. Clearly it had been shot on a shoestring, Melanie boasting that it had been made for a quarter of a million. As he watched the film, Marcus smiled, thinking if this travesty cost a quarter of a million, then what had they spent the money on? Location catering?

Almost eighty minutes into the film, Melanie noticed him sneaking a look at his watch, so he whispered reassuringly in her ear, 'All I want to see is you, my darling.'

She nodded and pointed at the screen. And there she was, playing a nurse. She had three lines of dialogue, and Marcus wanted to disappear he was so embarrassed. It wasn't that her movement was wooden, but her voice lacked fire. She had the most wooden, monotone voice of anyone he had ever heard on screen. He couldn't help wondering if she was aware of her own flat delivery of the lines, and what could he say to her after the film was over?

Thankfully the film ended a little after ninety-five minutes. Marcus kissed her cheek and said, 'Well done, my sweetheart. Terrific.'

She seemed satisfied with that. Her only disappointment was the way her fiancé rushed her out of the preview cinema afterwards, saying he had booked a table at Simpson's in The Strand, and he fancied something traditional and English, like roast beef and Yorkshire pudding. They walked down to Shaftesbury Avenue, where he hailed a cab, and forty-five minutes later, they sat opposite one another across a gleaming white tablecloth.

'So, what did you think of the film?' Melanie asked when the food arrived.

Marcus lacked diplomacy. Deliberately so. He considered himself a pragmatist and a plain talker. There was never any sense in hiding behind prevarication and pretence. Tell it like it is, was his motto.

'I thought you looked stunning, sweetheart. As a nurse, you'd raise my blood pressure. Believe me.' He laughed self-consciously before telling her what he really thought. 'But I'm sorry, I thought the film was a heap of shite.' Remembering the thought he'd had in the cinema, he smiled pompously and delivered the line with supercilious satisfaction. 'And if the budget was as much as a quarter of a million, I must ask myself: what did they spend the money on? Location catering?'

Melanie looked down thoughtfully at her slices of roast beef, cutting off small segments and pushing them round the plate. The way she toyed with her food began to irritate Marcus and he snapped, 'You didn't honestly think that was good, did you? I mean, what was the point of it? And no one got paid much, did they. Peanuts. What did they pay you? Remind me.'

She glared at him. 'You know very well how much. I told you.'

'A hundred quid for one day. Jesus! Was it worth it?'

'It's what it could lead to.'

He laughed harshly. 'Yeah, and I'll be next president of the USA.'

'Well, why not? You've got a lot in common with Donald Trump.'

Rather than taking it as an insult, he laughed delightedly and said, 'Touché!'

Despite feeling piqued about the film, because she knew Marcus was right, she nevertheless wanted him to flatter her – even if it meant lying a little. Having seen how her three lines made little impact, she felt fragile, and wanted him to boost her ego. It didn't matter that her performance was lack lustre, what she craved was his indulgence, like a child showing a parent a painting, wanting love not criticism. Although she had been his lover for two years, she knew they had been living a dream. Getting lost in cloud cuckoo land. Then, since witnessing something of his family life, the fiasco of his wife's funeral and argument with his daughters, she became aware of how heartless and unforgiving he could be. She wondered if he was capable of change. Could she turn him into a nicer person?

She washed a miniscule piece of roast potato down with a sip of claret, put down her glass and looked at him seriously. 'Marcus, d'you mind if I ask you something?'

'What is it?' he asked cautiously, mistakenly thinking she was about to ask him what he thought of her performance.

'Why are you cutting yourself off so completely from your daughters?'

'I would have thought that was obvious.'

'Not to me, it isn't. You've brought them into this world—'

'And provided for them, well into their twenties. And you saw how they've repaid me. I can't forgive them for the way they behaved at the rugby club. Never. It was unforgivable.'

120

'Are you sure this is not your ego that's been damaged? The fact that they showed you up in front of the other mourners.'

He aimed his dinner knife in her direction to make a point. 'I'll admit that was hurtful, yes. And it's hard to recover from a scene like that.'

'I'm sure you'll manage.'

'What's that supposed to mean?'

'It means I…oh, I don't know…I was hoping your daughters might eventually come at accept me.'

Marcus shook his head adamantly. 'You saw the sheer hatred Vanessa spewed at you. Do you honestly think she's capable of sweetness and light now? Well, I fucking don't. And I'll tell you this for nothing, Mel. Here's where the discussion ends about those two. Let's end this conversation now and talk about something else.'

'But you can't hate your own daughters that much. You can't.'

'As it happens, yes I can.'

Melanie sighed, then attempted to eat some of the beef. Suddenly she gagged, placed a hand over her mouth and stood up. Panicking, she said, 'I feel sick. Excuse me.'

She dashed off to the ladies, clutching her stomach. Marcus watched as she dashed through the restaurant and wondered if she would make the ladies loo in time. He looked round at some of the other diners who had witnessed his fiancée's agitated exit, but they mostly looked away, embarrassed.

But Marcus was hungry, and no amount of soul searching over his wretched family was going to put him off his dinner. He shovelled a large portion of beef with horseradish sauce into his mouth, and hoped he wouldn't get another attack of heartburn.

Seventeen

As Karen played the downtrodden wife, displaying for her husband's benefit a subservient demeanour in her body language, accepting wholeheartedly his ridiculous ambitions, she wondered if she went too far. But he appeared not to notice anything very different in her behaviour, and she knew his ego was boosted by her willingness to please him.

Having been out all day, he came home late and, as soon as he strutted into the living room, he was so ridiculously pleased with himself she could imagine him beating his chest. She asked him where he had been and knew he was lying as he boasted about a producers' meeting for the film, especially as he was done up in suit and tie instead of his smart casual image.

Usually, he was meticulous about his attire, and if he removed his suit jacket he would always take it into the bedroom and hang it up in the wardrobe. But not tonight. Tonight was different, she noticed. When he took off his jacket, he threw it uncaringly onto one of the easy chairs.

'How about a drink?' he suggested.

'I think you may have had a few already, Paul,' she replied. Then, not wanting it to sound like a criticism, added, 'So you can pour me a large one. I've got a bit of catching up to do.'

He smiled, and she recognised that all powerful confidence, and the indifferent cruelty it masked. But now she knew about his past. That report had been explicit, and it altered the way she looked at him. Watching his every move. Analysing.

He poured two large brandy nightcaps and came and sat close to her on the sofa. She thought she recognised the signals, that controlling glint in his eye, telling her he was about to bestow on her his love benediction, giving her the pleasure he thought she desired. But tonight, though, was slightly different. She could tell he wanted to satisfy his own desires, could see he was aroused, and guessed the arousal came from another source.

As soon as the brandy glasses were empty, he began kissing her. Then he took her right hand and placed it on his penis. Through the material of his trousers, she squeezed and kneaded, feeling the stiffness of his erection. Then, just as he was about to take the foreplay to another level, he brushed her hand away. She looked him in the eye, wanting to know why she couldn't please him, but he just took her other hand, pulled her up from the sofa and guided her towards the bedroom.

As she undressed she thought about the way he had pushed her hand away, as if he saw it as a weakness. A loss of control. In the bedroom, he always had to be the master not the slave. And she guessed that his lovemaking would be studied and controlled, performing like an automaton, as he usually did. But as she slid into bed beside him, she was surprised at the level of his arousal, the way his body shuddered with the anticipation of intercourse. She guessed that for the first time in bed together, he had become aware that this loss power was a deficiency, and would resent her for it. His stiff penis was pressed hard against her thigh, and he moved away from her, trying to regain some of that precious control.

Attempting to recover his usual manipulative fornication methods, he began kneading her breasts as he tried to control his own lechery. But whereas in the past she had been beguiled by his carnal proficiency, this time it was very different. She felt the start of a panic attack. She was reminded of that detective's report, the details about the accusation of murder in North Wales. His wife, fighting for breath. Sucking in water. Drowning. While his fingernails dug into her, pushing her under.

As Paul kissed her nipples, and ran a hand up the inside of her thigh – a hand that now seemed unnaturally large and threatening – she stiffened with fear. How could she go through with this lovemaking, knowing how that woman had drowned under the hands that grabbed her legs now? Terrible, vicious hands. Hands capable of murder.

Thankfully, his arousal was so great that not long after he entered her, he climaxed in less than thirty seconds, and she felt his penis become flaccid almost immediately. For the first time in their lovemaking he seemed glad it was over so quickly, relieved that he had ejaculated something that controlled him out of his system.

He mumbled a resentful 'goodnight', then rolled over and went to sleep. She lay on her back, eyes wide open, staring at the shifting shadows of the ceiling. Then she heard his gentle breathing and guessed he had fallen into a deep, alcohol-induced sleep.

Unable to sleep herself, she thought about the way he touched her, and she shuddered with fear, imagining his hands around her throat. Large, slaughtering hands as she had seen on those ancient Greek gravestones in a museum in Madrid. She had been awed by the representation of power in those sword-wielding mythical Homeric heroes who had no mercy or pity for their enemies. Later, when she was at art college, she studied the ancient Greek and Roman artefacts in the British Museum, and she remembered those stones and being influenced by their depiction of oversized, omnipotent hands, but only as a way of improving her designs in an abstract way.

Now she hated and feared those ancient Greek stories, as the horror of death reared its hideous head and became all too real.

Eventually, after what seemed like hours of mind-debilitating insomnia, but was only forty-five minutes, she fell into a deep sleep.

Rough hands shook her awake. Large killer hands grabbing her shoulders

'Darling! What's the matter?'

It was Paul, shaking her out of a bad dream. Images fled from her brain as she tried to recall the horror of the nightmare. She knew death had been rampant in her head, bombarding her with pictures of slaughter.

After she had calmed down, the nightmare fizzled out, so that she was left wondering what she had said.

'I think you were having a nightmare,' he said. 'Can you remember what it was about?'

'I don't know,' she replied groggily. 'What did I say? Did I say anything?'

'Nothing coherent. You were just shouting, like someone was attacking you.'

Relieved she had given nothing away about knowing of his murderous past, she lied, making up a vague story about being chased by a mythical demon.

For the remainder of the night, she drifted into a trouble-free sleep. In the morning, she found Paul gone, and a note in the kitchen saying he had business to attend to and would be gone for most of the day.

She smiled and relaxed. Now she was past caring.

Eighteen

Two stops beyond Stratford on the Central Line, Paul got off the train at Snaresbrook as Terry Lennox had instructed him, and followed the ex-gangster's directions into Hollybush Hill to meet him at the Eagle public house.

As he walked into the pub, Paul spotted Lennox standing at the bar, sipping gin and tonic. He looked more like a theatrical impresario than a gangster, in his light blue suit and multi-coloured silk tie with horizontal stripes. Although he was seventy-years-old, Lennox looked remarkably young for his years, with a trim figure, a good head of wavy grey hair, and a lean face with dark brown eyes.

'What you having, young man?' Lennox asked as they shook hands.

'I'm hot and thirsty after that journey. I'll have a pint of San Miguel.'

When he caught the barmaid's attention, Lennox asked her to put another Bombay gin in his glass and ordered Paul his pint. 'Let's sit out in the garden, where we can talk,' he said, after they'd been served..

While they sat at a table in the garden, Lennox studied Paul carefully, his eyes narrowing slightly. 'So why did you want to see me privately, on my home turf? Is something wrong with the movie project? You come to tell me you want out, and you're trying to let me down gently? Is that it?'

Paul wanted to say it was Lennox's idea to meet close to where he lived but thought better of it. Instead, he shook his head rapidly and replied, 'No, the film's still on the cards.'

'Good. Cos I'd hate to think after all the work we put in to it—'

It crossed Paul's mind that if he chose to back out of the project there might be a nasty penalty to pay. He knew the gangster was determined to get his picture made, his last legacy and fifteen minutes of fame rather than notoriety. To reassure Lennox, he feigned enthusiasm, beaming congenially. 'Things can only get better,' he crowed. 'Much better. Soon I might be able to up the budget. Which means...' he tapped a finger on the wooden table to emphasise his point... 'we could attract a bigger name.'

'That's what I like to hear, Paul. But I still don't get it. Why this secret meeting with yours truly then?'

125

Paul glanced around the garden furtively, afraid someone might eavesdrop on their conversation, although the nearest bench to where they sat was empty; as it was only just gone twelve the lunchtime rush hadn't started.

'You seem a bit nervous,' the gangster observed. 'Like some of the customers that come to this place. A good many of the clientele who use this pub have a good reason to be nervous.'

Thrown into sudden confusion, Paul frowned. 'How d'you mean? I'm not with you.'

Lennox tilted his head to an overweight man in a cheap suit, two tables away from them, who appeared to be suffering with every mouthful of beer he took. He also had a large whisky chaser, which Paul saw him knock back nervously.

'See that geezer there? That could be his last drop of booze for a year or more.' Lennox jerked a thumb towards the main road. 'That building down the road, on the opposite side – that's Snaresbrook Crown Court. Some of the afternoon cases'll come in here to snatch a few bevvies before they're sentenced. It could be their last drink for some time. Yeah, this place will be heaving soon, with solicitors and barristers, and the lucky bastards who got away with it in the morning session. But most of the sad bastards you see in here when the pub opens are making the most of it before they go down. Those who aren't on remand, of course.'

'You told me this is your local,' Paul said with a knowing smile. 'So why d'you use this pub?'

'Apart from it being a half mile walk from where I live, I like to come here to remind myself that there but for the grace of God—' He nodded at the man two tables away and laughed.

'I suppose you can count yourself lucky.'

'No. Luck has nothing to do with it. I was always smarter than the others. Careful. And never greedy. Worked my firm like a proper firm, if you know what I mean. Now let's get down to business. When you said you wanted to see me, but not Richie, our director, right away I thought to myself, there's got to be something dodgy going on.'

'Well, not really.'

Lennox raised his eyebrows in mock surprise. 'No?'

'Nothing that affects the film, I mean.'

'So, what are you after?'

'I want to buy something and I don't know how to go about buying it.'

126

Lennox smirked. 'Something illegal, eh? Which is why you thought you'd come to your Uncle Terry.'

'You guessed it. I need a firearm.'

Lennox laughed. 'Just like that. Walk into my local and you want to buy a shooter.'

'I thought you might know someone who—'

'Hang about,' Lennox cut in, then swallowed a mouthful of his drink while he pointed a finger at Paul. 'This why you told me you can up the budget for the film? You going to rob a bank?'

'Of course not. And I can't tell you why I need it. I just thought because of the gangster film, and because you could probably put your hands on—'

Lennox slammed his glass down. 'Supposing I can. Whatever you use it for, I've got to know what happens to it afterwards. It's not like the US, you know. Guns can be more easily traced in the UK.'

'I can promise you this, Terry, if you can get me a firearm, it will disappear after it's been used. That I can promise you.'

'And how will this shooter up the budget on the movie if it ain't a robbery?'

'Just trust me on this. It's better that you don't know.'

Lennox was silent, studying Paul thoroughly while he made up his mind. After a long pause, he said, 'Let's just suppose I can get you a shooter, and some ammunition, how do I know you won't get caught in whatever it is you're planning?'

'There's no way you'll be implicated, Terry.'

'No? And if you're interrogated by the Filth, how can I be sure you won't tell them where you got the shooter from?'

Paul grinned uncertainly, unsure of how Lennox might take his next rationalisation. 'Put it this way,' he began, carefully choosing his words, 'if I was unlucky enough to get caught – which I am confident is not going to happen – and I ended up inside, I would be stupid to implicate you, wouldn't I?'

'Oh? And why is that, Paul?'

'I think you might have colleagues serving time, and those loyal subjects of yours could get at me.'

Lennox chuckled heartily as if he'd been told a good joke, then shook his head. 'I think you've been seeing too many gangster movies.'

'But you see my point,' Paul insisted. 'There is no way I would dare to risk involving you in my…my scheme. And if you can't help me, Terry, maybe you can put me in touch with someone who can.'

'I never said I couldn't help you. I just need to be sure you won't do nothing stupid and I end up in this pub one day – like that fat git over there – wondering if I'll go down for something as banal as providing you with a shooter.'

'That's not going to happen, believe me.'

'Got it all worked out, have you? The perfect crime?'

Thinking the gangster was being sarcastic, Paul leant forward and lowered his voice. 'I have the perfect alibi. And there is no way my alibi will want to go down as an accessory. All I need is a firearm. With a silencer.'

'You ever fired a gun before?'

'No. Never.'

'Well, I guess you won't miss if you get close enough to your victim to commit the murder.'

'I never said anything about murder.'

'You didn't have to. If it was a robbery, and you fired the gun in the air, you'd want a lot of noise to put the frighteners on people. But a silencer means just one thing. Murder.'

Paul knocked back most of his beer as he thought about his next exchange with Lennox. 'Listen, Mark, if this gives us the dosh to make this picture, what do you care where the money comes from?'

'True,' the gangster said with a smile. 'If that's the case, I'll get you a shooter, silencer and ammo for five hundred notes. OK?'

'It's a deal. And will it work?'

'Will what work?'

'The firearm. I presume it will have been used in the past. Only you hear of guns jamming sometimes. If that happened I'd be really up shit creek.'

'Trust me. It won't jam.'

'Well, I know bugger all about guns—'

'That figures. Do yourself a favour. If you're worried about it, buy yourself a lottery ticket for next Saturday's draw.'

'What's that go to do with it?'

'Because that gun will have as much chance of jamming as you winning the jackpot. So, quit worrying. And if it's a pistol I get you, pick up the ejected casings afterwards and get rid of them. And I guess you're hoping if it's got a silencer it works like a James Bond film. That's a complete myth. It will still sound like a car back firing. It only goes down from around 160 decibels to 130.'

Paul thought about the size of his father-in-law's house and shook his head. 'I don't think it'll be a problem.'

'Good. And there is just one more thing.'

'What's that, Mark?

The gangster pushed his glass towards Paul. 'It's your round. I'll have a large Bombay and slimline.'

*

Marcus was on edge. A deal of his had gone sour and he also felt agitated because Melanie insisted on meeting him for lunch in the self-service cafeteria of the Oxford Street branch of Marks and Spencer's. Not his sort of place at all. She was already seated at a table when he arrived and eating what looked like a syrupy flapjack with a side salad, and drinking a cup of hot chocolate overflowing with cream. He kissed her briefly on the cheek and looked at his watch.

'Sorry, darling, I haven't got long. What made you pick this place?'

He made it sound as if she had suggested meeting in a homeless squat, so she smiled sweetly and said, 'I thought it might remind you of your humble origins. But even you must admit, sweetheart, it's not exactly slumming it.'

He looked over at the self-service counter and scowled. 'And I have to serve my bloody self.'

'Oh, go on. Don't be such an old grump. Go and get a sandwich and coffee.'

Beaming at him, she looked so radiant, that he melted under her gaze and quipped, 'OK. But not so much of the old.'

When he returned with a prawn and mayonnaise sandwich and an Americano coffee, she smiled sweetly, and he noticed the way she looked worried and pleased at the same time.

'What made you pick this place?' he asked.

'I wanted to look at some clothes which I might need.'

'For next week's holiday?'

'Not, not for our holiday. More for the future. December, probably.'

'I've heard of early Christmas shopping but not the first week in June.'

She looked at him, restraining a smile, but wrinkling her nose to look deliberately cute. Then she said, 'I wanted to look at the maternity wear.'

'You what?'

'Sweetheart, I went to the doctor's first thing this morning. I'm definitely pregnant.'

'Pregnant?' he repeated.

'Yes, we're going to have a baby. I hope you're pleased. I couldn't bear it if you—'

He reached across the table and grabbed her hand. 'Sorry! Of course I'm pleased. It just came out of the blue that's all. It was a delayed reaction. That's fantastic, Mel.'

'Are you sure? I was worried you might not want it.'

'Don't be silly, Mel. I'm delighted. Christ! We must have a celebration tonight.'

'Well, I don't think I'll be drinking. Not now.'

'I wonder if you've got a little bloke in there.'

'Is that what you want? A boy?'

He shrugged and smiled. 'I don't mind. Although, I must admit, a boy would be good. Because I've already got two daughters.'

Melanie, looking sombre, shook her head disapprovingly. 'Don't you mean you *had* two daughters?'

'Yeah. Thanks for reminding me. And that will seem like something that happened to someone else in another life. Now it's time to move on. And this time it'll be different, I promise you. We'll bring this child of ours into the world with heaps of love.'

'And not make the same mistakes you made with your other children.'

He frowned deeply. 'Maybe it is my fault, turning those two into ungrateful monsters. But, like I said, I don't have a time machine and I can't go back and change things. That's why I will do things properly this time.'

He began eating his sandwich hungrily, then she saw him glancing surreptitiously at his watch.

'Slow down, Marcus. You don't want to get another attack of heartburn again. The last one was terrible. I thought you were going to die.'

'I'll be all right. I forget to take my pill that time. I'm fine now,' he mumbled through a mouthful of sandwich.

130

His fiancée stretched forward and wiped a smear of mayonnaise off his cheek with a napkin. 'Look at you. You need to slow down, darling. Otherwise you'll get stressed out.'

'I'm just finishing some deals this week, so we can relax during our week in Paris.
You sure you're OK to travel?'

'I'll be fine. It's not like we're flying. I've heard that can sometimes be a problem in the early stages of pregnancy.'

'Yeah,' he said. 'Must be something to do with the pressurised cabin.'

He wolfed down the rest of the sandwich, gulped his coffee, gave a tiny belch and said, 'That's it. Sorry to leave you so quickly but I've got some problems to sort out. I'll ring you later and we can see about tonight's celebration.'

He rose hastily, kissed her on the lips, then departed. She watched him weaving his way through the tables, and expected him to turn back and wave from the exit, but he carried on walking as though he had dismissed her from his mind already, and was elsewhere making deals.

She frowned thoughtfully, thinking about the hatred between Marcus and his daughters, and how poisoned those relationships had become. She hoped and prayed that history would not repeat itself where his new family was concerned.

Nineteen

Noticing how quiet Vanessa was, Paul guessed she was thinking about the death of her father, and decided to keep quiet himself rather than intrude on her thoughts. If she changed her mind at this late stage he would go ballistic, especially after all that last-minute planning.

Wanting to keep a clear head, he sipped strong black coffee as he sat at her pine table, going over everything in his head again. Aiming to go unnoticed by anyone dashing home from work in this district, he was dressed in dark blue denims, a short-sleeved blue shirt, and nondescript black lace-up shoes. This was the first part of the plan, leaving the flat around five in the evening, drawing no attention to himself.

Having parked the BMW where Vanessa suggested, and following their arrangement to row as he left the flat on Saturday afternoon when she returned from the sandwich bar, he planned to inadvertently set the alarm off on the car as he was about to leave, drawing further attention to his presence in the district, and looking guilty because he was not supposed to be at his wife's sister's place.

Seated opposite him, across the table, Vanessa sipped wine to steady her nerves. He realised she needed the drink, but he worried about her driving erratically and getting stopped by the police. What if they were searched? Inside the backpack at his feet was not only the change of clothing, but the pistol. A Glock 19. Lennox had shown him how to attach the silencer, a left-hand thread, which would take up valuable time when he entered the house, so it was already attached, the pistol and silencer taking up about a foot of space in the bag.

'I wouldn't drink more than the one glass,' he said. 'Just in case we're stopped by the police. You being breathalysed and failing is all we need at this stage.'

'I'll be fine,' she shrugged. 'Besides, the roads'll be busy on a Friday evening.'

'No more fucking booze,' he yelled.

She was taken aback by the sudden change; but when she thought about it, it wasn't because of the raised voice, or even the viciousness of his

132

delivery, but because of the expletive. It was the first time she noticed him swearing and it took her by surprise.

'OK,' she agreed. 'Just this one, then I'll knock it on the head.'

'Make sure you do,' he warned. 'I don't want you over the limit when I get back from Richmond. It'll be near to pubs' closing time and I don't want to risk getting stopped.'

'You're right.' She stood up, carried the glass into the kitchen and poured it into the sink. When she returned and sat at the table, he acknowledged her gesture with a nod. They were both silent, thinking about what lay ahead.

To break the oppressive silence, she said, 'I checked the light bulbs in the Mini. They all work perfectly, so we can't be stopped for that.'

'The mobiles, I take it, are fully charged.'

'Hundred per cent.' She laughed nervously. 'I mean, they're only being used for your one call. Although, I think you ought to text me rather than call me from Richmond Station. And I'll return your text. It would be better than calling, just in case someone overhears you.'

'Good point. And, as agreed, we remove the SIM cards, chuck them somewhere obscure, then smash up the phones and get rid of them.'

Paul looked at his watch. 'It's ten to five. We may as well make a move. No point in hanging around for another ten minutes.'

Vanessa felt numb. This was it. What they had discussed was about to become a reality. Part of her wanted to stop it; call it off. But in another part of her that was buried deep inside, there skulked a thrusting curiosity, a terrible demon determined to test her, to see if she was capable of murder. Her own father. And yet, all she saw was a monster, and her hatred boiled like poison in a cauldron as she thought of his infidelity. And then there was that night, when she was only ten-years-old and he came into her room. She shuddered every time she remembered what he made her do, and she could never seem to wash her hands clean after that, or drive out the smell that she could still imagine. It happened only the one time, but it was enough for her to fear him. And she had always wondered if he had done the same to her sister.

Paul stood up and shouldered his backpack. The ripples in Vanessa's stomach were like uncoordinated waves as she followed him to the door. Her breathing shallow, she wondered if she might faint if she didn't catch her breath. She shut the front door quietly, and they both hurried to her Mini which was parked about fifty yards further along the street.

133

The street wasn't busy; just a few people hurrying home from work, who barely glanced at them.

They drove towards Chiswick High Road, and then headed towards Hammersmith. Just before Ravenscourt Park, Vanessa looked in the mirror and saw there was a police car right behind them. Was it her imagination? Or were they being followed?

'Shit!' she hissed.

'What's wrong?'

'Don't look round…I said, don't look round. There's a police car right behind us.'

'Try not to panic. We've done nothing wrong. It's just a coincidence they're behind us.'

Paul resisted the urge to look round, and they continued in silence, tension in the air like electricity, with Vanessa looking in the mirror every so often. When they got into the one-way system near Hammersmith Broadway, the police car overtook them.

'I told you,' Paul said. 'Nothing to worry about.' But she heard him blowing out his breath in relief.

She pulled in and parked beyond a bus stop. Paul grabbed the rucksack from the back seat and got out. 'See you at the Ravenscourt Park rendezvous,' he said, and waited for her to say something before closing the door. But she just nodded, and he guessed that wishing someone luck in this situation was hardly appropriate. He shut the door, and she indicated and pulled out into the traffic. He stood on the pavement and watched her drive off. He was committed now. No turning back. He felt nervous and excited, never having fired a gun before, or a 'shooter' as he remembered Lennox calling it. This was out of his comfort zone. Whereas the others had been accidents, he didn't like having to rely on a mechanical device. Again, he recalled that scene in *Schindler's List* where a Nazi officer attempts to shoot a concentration camp victim and his Luger wouldn't fire, and was chilled by the thoughts of what might happen if he confronted his father-in-law with no back up, no way of ending the bastard's life if the gun failed. He relied solely on the Glock, and he hoped it was more reliable than that Nazi thug's Luger, which tormented him with images of the only thing that might go wrong with this perfect crime. He hoped Lennox was right about the odds against the Glock jamming.

A clock on a Hammersmith Broadway building told him it was 5.45. Knowing he had a lot of time to kill, he walked to the Underground station entrance to pick up a free copy of the *Evening Standard*. He then sauntered into King Street and found the William Morris, a Wetherspoon's pub. He guessed it would be busy on a Friday evening, and he was right. The pub was heaving, and he congratulated himself for his choice of venue. So far so good. No one would give him a second glance. He would be the perfect non-entity here.

He went up to the bar, and had to wait almost ten minutes to get served, it was that busy. But he didn't mind. It was only 5.50, so he had more than two hours to kill. When he eventually caught a barman's eye, he ordered a pint of bitter shandy. Then, having stood at the bar for another ten minutes, he noticed a couple about to vacate a small table with two chairs. He hurried over and plonked his glass onto the table to commandeer it before anyone else. Then he sat and buried his head in the paper, sipping his drink ever so slowly, determined to make it last almost two hours, afraid alcohol might impair his performance. And he thought of the night's escapade as nothing more than another performance, with him as its star. The one in control, with a determination to win this one whatever the tragic consequences for those two women. For him it would be third time lucky.

Not that he'd been unlucky in his previous attempts to hit the jackpot. The murder trial in North Wales had been a bit of a glitch. But that's all it was. A glitch. He had got away with it, although the cost of his legal representation meant the money was soaked up by those bastard sponges in the legal profession.

As he sat, flicking over pages of the *Standard*, none of it registered. His brain was too busy imagining the successful outcome of everything he had worked towards. All the hours spent planning and scheming would be worth it. Soon, once the problem of the twins' father had been dealt with, he'd be rolling in it, and when the film was made, welcoming doors would always open for him.

At just gone seven o'clock, he had drunk only half of the pint, but none of the staff in this overcrowded pub bothered him or even noticed how slowly he drank. He realised he could probably spin the pint out for longer if he chose, but now it was just an hour and fifteen minutes until he needed to prepare for this perfect crime.

Details. That's what mattered. And he had everything covered.

At ten past eight, he didn't bother to down the last quarter pint of the sickly sweet shandy, and left to go to the toilet, taking his backpack with

135

him. He went into one of the cubicles and changed into the clothes in the backpack, taking care to remove the Glock with its deadly-looking silencer and laying it carefully across the top of the cistern. Because his wallet contained cards which could identify him, he had left it in the glove compartment of the BMW. All he had in the pocket of the denims was two-hundred pounds in cash, which he transferred to the right hand pocket of the track suit bottoms. Once he had stuffed the black shoes, denims and short-sleeved shirt in the backpack, he slid the gun in beside them, then checked the side pockets of the backpack for the other items he needed: surgical gloves and the key to the Richmond house. He transferred the gloves into the left pocket and the key to the right pocket with the money, securing both pockets with the zip. Finally, he put the Nike baseball cap on his head with it tilted low over his forehead, then left the pub, heading for Hammersmith Underground station.

*

When he came out of Richmond station, he kept his head down, just in case CCTV was checked following the crime. But even if they managed to capture on TV this man in trainers, track suit bottoms, cheap T-shirt and baseball cap, he doubted whether he could be recognised. Not only would they be unable to see who was under the peak of the baseball cap, but everyone who knew him would testify that he was always a snazzy dresser, and wouldn't be seen dead in this chav get-up. Although, he had serious doubts it would ever come to searching CCTV on Richmond station, or between there and Richmond Green. And even if they did, he told himself, just keep your head down and don't feel tempted to look up to search for any CCTV cameras.

As he walked past Richmond Theatre, he heard a burst of laughter followed by a ripple of applause, but didn't give it a thought, so intent was he on his operation. He kept walking determinedly and cut across the Green. He saw an elderly man walking a Yorkshire terrier heading towards him, so he stepped off the path and took a wide detour on the grass to avoid him, hoping the man might think it was someone wary of dogs and nothing more.

As he neared the house, he slipped the rucksack off his back and held it by one strap on his right shoulder. Before crossing the road from the

136

Green to the house, he stopped walking and took the surgical gloves from the left side pocket and stretched them over his hands.

As he crossed the pavement he got the key out of his pocket, then walked the short distance along to narrow drive to the front door, knowing he had only seconds before his father-in-law heard his entrance, demanded to know who it was, then came pounding downstairs to confront him. He unzipped the top of the rucksack, ready to grab the gun quickly.

Lennox had explained about the Glock having three safety mechanisms, but because the pistol was used by police in so many countries, an inner lever contained in the trigger, gave it the speed that was an advantage to so many police officers, and allowed a gunman to activate the trigger immediately, so the gun could be fired without having to worry about any external safety catches.

Taking a deep breath, he slid the key into the lock, heard it click and pushed the door open. As soon as he was inside, he slammed it shut, took the gun out of the bag, leaving the bag on the floor.

'Hello? Who the fuck is that?' came the indignant sound of his father-in-law from upstairs. 'Mel? Is that you? I thought I told you I don't ever want to be disturbed on a Friday.'

Paul walked quickly along the hall and into the kitchen at the back. He thought the sound of the pistol shot was less likely, despite the silencer, to be heard from the back of the house. He heard his father-in-law's angry footsteps pounding down the stairs. He waited to the left of the door, out of sight.

Silence. He imagined his father-in-law had reached the bottom of the stairs.

'What the fuck is going on?'

It sounded as if his father-in-law had spotted the backpack. It was time to deliver the nasty surprise.

'In the kitchen, Marcus. Say hello to your son-in-law.'

He heard the hurried shuffle of shoes on carpet as his father-in-law came bounding towards the kitchen. As he entered, he sensed Paul's presence and turned, anger and confusion spread across his face, his brain scrambling for a clue to what was happening. And then Paul raised the gun. His father-in-law opened his mouth to say something, but there was a terrific whip crack noise as Paul pulled the trigger. Although he had aimed straight for the heart, the barrel jumped and the bullet caught his father-in-law at the edge of his left shoulder. Presumably he felt no pain yet; only the sudden shock of what was happening, because Marcus Bradshaw looked surprised and confused, though deep in his eyes was an expression of horror. Then Paul held the gun steady, aiming for the centre of the chest. The bullet hit his father-in-law right in the centre, but had probably missed his heart. Paul stepped closer, the gun only inches away from his victim. Still Marcus Bradshaw remained standing, his back against the doorframe, as if he still hadn't registered any pain, and his body wouldn't collapse until it had.

'Goodbye, Daddy,' Paul sneered as he held the gun only a foot away from his father-in-law's head, then pulled the trigger. Another loud crack. This time an enormous hole appeared in Marcus Bradshaw's forehead, the impact of the missile slammed his body back through the doorway into the hall, and a stream of blood burst from the back of his head, spattering strings of red across the cream carpet.

Paul walked forward a few paces to observe the damage and to make certain his victim was dead, careful to avoid treading in any blood from the other two wounds. He waited a moment, frozen by the enormity of his actions, awed and transfixed, unable to move a muscle but aware of the sudden silence in the house following the loud report of the three shots. Lennox had been right. The sound guns with silencers make in the movies was a complete myth, and he feared someone in the street outside may have heard the shots.

He stared at the body, almost smiling, glad his father-in-law had a moment to reflect on his imminent death. How Paul had enjoyed that look of fear in the man's eyes, his soul given a fraction of time to smell death.

Shaking himself out of his moment of triumph, Paul knew he needed to get out of that house as quickly as possible, just in case someone had heard the shots and telephoned the police. First, he needed to grab the ejected casings. They had ejected in an arc to his right, two of them landing on the work surface, but one of them had ricocheted off a shelf and gone under the refectory table to his left. He stooped quickly to pick it up, then retrieved the casings from the work surface, shoving all three ejected cartridges into the left pocket of his track suit, and zipped it up. Then, carefully avoiding the body and any blood splatters, he went into the hallway, hurried up the stairs, and threw open doors hurriedly until he found his father-in-law's study. Vanessa had told him that the CCTV camera trained on the front door was housed in a cupboard next to a built-in bookcase. Wasting no time, he threw open the door, and checked the monitor. It wasn't switched on; the monitor was a blank screen.

He laughed and spoke aloud. 'Thank you, Marcus. You've been a great help.'

Hurrying downstairs, he put the gun into the rucksack, picked it up, holding it with one strap on his right shoulder, opened the door and left the house. He walked briskly towards Old Palace Lane, turned the corner and headed towards the river, removing the surgical gloves as he walked along and stopped briefly to put them into one of the side pockets of the rucksack. Passing the White Swan, he saw it was busy, and was relieved to see only two people standing outside having a smoke, and they were so deeply involved in a discussion they barely glanced in his direction. But when he reached the river, and rounded the corner onto the towpath, he almost bumped into a tall, skinny man walking an ancient spaniel that could barely walk. The man bade him a good evening and, keeping his head down, he mumbled a brief reply before slowing down and walking casually to give the appearance that he may have been someone on their way to the pub further up the riverside. Glancing back over his shoulder, he saw the man turning the corner into Old Palace Lane, so he hurried along the towpath in the direction of Richmond Bridge. In the distance, he spotted a group of four people, two young couples, coming towards him. He almost panicked, needing to get rid of the gun before they got any nearer. They were at least two hundred yards away, but even if they saw him chucking something into the Thames, they couldn't possibly see what it was in the twilight. He stood near to the edge of the river, took the gun out of his bag, hurled it as far as he could, and heard the splash as it fell somewhere in the middle of the river. Glancing sideways, he noticed the two couples were walking rapidly towards him and were perhaps only a hundred yards away now. He fumbled in his left-side pocket containing the bullet casings, managed to grab hold of just two of the casings and threw them as hard as he could. Being much lighter than the gun, one landed in the river only about a foot away from the bank, but the other fell short and landed on the bank at the edge of the water. He could see it glinting in the semi-darkness, lodged between blades of grass and a stone. There was no way he could leave it there. Christ! Having removed the gloves, his prints were on that casing now. He had to get it back.

He heard the couples approaching, talking and laughing. Standing perched on the edge of the bank, looking at the river, his back to the towpath, he heard the footsteps of the couples as they passed by, and could feel them staring at him, silent now, probably curious as to why this yob in a baseball cap was staring at the dark waters of the Thames. He let them get a hundred yards further along, just before the turning into Old Palace Lane, and knew he would have to lie on the towpath and see if he could reach over and grab the casing. But then, when he looked towards Richmond Bridge, he saw another dog-walker heading towards him. His brain crystal clear now as the adrenaline boosted his resolve, he lay down on the concrete and reached over the edge of the bank. He could just about touch the casing with the tips of his fingers, but however hard he stretched his arm and hand, he was unable to get a hold on it. And he could hear the man getting nearer, and the sniffing of the dog. The only option left to him was to try to dislodge the casing by flicking it, hoping it would hit the water and sink. He flicked it with his index finger, but it remained stubbornly lodged behind the blade of grass. He heard the panting of the dog now as it approached. Another giant effort as he strained and stretched his hand, folded back his index finger then flicked hard, so hard he felt the spasm through his fingernail. But he was relieved to see the casing shoot into the water and disappear.

He got hurriedly to his feet. The middle-aged man had stopped while his dog cocked its leg, and he stared at Paul, who felt he had to give some sort of explanation. Keeping his head low, hoping the peak of the baseball cap kept his features in shadow, he mumbled, 'All that trouble to get a two-pound coin.' Fortunately, the man laughed, and replied, 'Which will only get you half a pint these days.'

The dog having finished its business, the man walked on, leaving Paul to wonder if he might come forward as a witness once the body was discovered. Not that it mattered. Paul had the perfect, watertight alibi, and his disguise as a lout in a baseball cap might be dismissed as just someone behaving strangely and nothing to do with the murder.

As he hurried past the White Cross Hotel, up into Water Lane, he realised he still had to get rid of the remaining casing and the key. Maybe down a drain, the first one he came to. But it was a warm Friday night, and Richmond was busy. Much too busy to be seen dropping something down a drain. As he hurried along George Street towards the station, he knew it was a lost opportunity. He wasn't thinking straight. He should have improvised. Gone up onto Richmond Bridge and dropped the key and casing into the river from there.

Still, what did it really matter? He was nearly at the station. He could get rid of them down a drain in a back street at Ravenscourt Park, where it would be quiet. Using his Oyster card – the one he'd bought with cash – he went through the barrier and onto the platform. There was a train about to leave in five minutes. Before getting on it, he stood on the platform, and having committed Vanessa's new mobile number to memory, he sent her a text, saying, 'Job done. Train leaves Richmond in 5 mins.'

He got on the train in a middle carriage, and sat with his head down, staring at his mobile phone screen. He almost smiled at something he should have realised earlier. That would have been the perfect way to walk along unnoticed, texting on his mobile, like so many people obsessed with their precious devices.

The mobile gave a gentle bleep, indicating a text. It was Vanessa's communication which read, 'Good. See you in 20 minutes.' He clicked off the phone and relaxed. He was almost home and dry. Even if witnesses came forward following the discovery of the body, he had the perfect alibi, and there was no way Vanessa was going to back out. It was a perfect crime. Now all he had to do was get rid of all the clothing, the key and the bullet casing.

There were about a half dozen other passengers in his carriage. It was one of the newer walk-through District Line trains, and could be walked from one end of the train to the other. Sitting opposite him was the inevitable unkempt and unbalanced woman he could see was itching to start a banal conversation. He tried not to look at her and kept staring at his phone. But this didn't deter her. She was determined to involve him in her observations.

'Very useful these trains,' she began. And when he didn't respond, she leant forward, peering at him under the brim of his cap. 'I say, these trains, they're new you know. You always had separate carriages before. You forget, don't you. You always forget.'

The train rumbled into Kew station, so pretending he had to get off, he walked forwards along through the dividing corridor into the next carriage, and sat down again.

It took another ten minutes to get to Ravenscourt Park. He was the only passenger to get off at this stop, and as he was five minutes early he walked unhurriedly down from the overground platform to the station exit below, then turned right into Ravenscourt Road, and a little further along, right again into Flora Gardens. By now, half an hour had lapsed since

Vanessa's text. He hoped she wouldn't be long. The street was so quiet, he worried that if someone spotted him hanging around, they might report him as someone loitering with intent.

He walked along the street, which curved to the left, and just past the bend in the pavement he found a drain. He took the casing and key out of each pocket, wiped them free of prints on a corner of his T-shirt – just as an added precaution – and dropped them between the slots in the drain. He heard a slight chink as they hit something solid, not very far below, but he didn't think that mattered. What were the chances of anyone finding these items soon and linking them to the murder of Marcus Bradshaw?

Returning to the corner of the street, he waited nervously as he checked his watch again. It was nearly half ten. Thirty-four minutes had gone by since her text. Still, her timing had been an estimate, he reasoned. Where driving through traffic was concerned, no one can accurately predict an arrival time.

Someone walking up Ravenscourt Road stared at him, probably wondering what a man wearing a baseball cap was doing loitering in a residential area this late. He wished she would hurry up. Perhaps she'd had an accident. Or the car wouldn't start. Christ! Everything depended on the alibi and getting back to her place.

And then he realised what may have happened. She needed to pick up a couple of bottles of wine at an off-licence as they had arranged, and she probably got held up in a queue. But as he waited, panic started to set in. Forty minutes had passed since her text and there was still no sign of her. Nor in the next five minutes.

Although they had agreed to make just the one text call, he dialled her number. He had to know where she was and what was happening. He held the phone close to his ear and waited while it clicked into ringing mode. Instead, an automatic voice informed him: 'The number you have dialled is unavailable.'

Fuck! What was happening? How the hell was he supposed to get back to her place?

Panicking now, he walked down Ravenscourt Road towards the busy main road, and stood on the corner, looking in the direction of Chiswick for any sign of her approaching car. He wondered if he was conspicuous now, and could be picked up by any CCTV cameras.

His agitation increased as streams of approaching traffic, some cars blinding him with headlights, cruised by, and still there was no sign of her.

Checking the time, he saw that fifty minutes had elapsed since her text message. Something had gone horribly wrong. And why didn't she answer her mobile? He rang it again and got the same message, telling him the number dialled was unavailable.

Seeing a black cab coming along on the opposite side of the road, with its hire light on, he raised his arm impulsively and yelled 'Taxi!' He knew it was a stupid thing to do, the driver would be sure to remember the man in the baseball cap, carrying a rucksack, who was picked up in Ravenscourt Park and taken to Vanessa's place. He would have to choose a different address, but he couldn't remember any of the other street names, other than the one where he had parked the BMW. But he did remember that she lived not far from Gunnersbury, her nearest station. At least it was a location to give the driver that was unmemorable, hopefully.

Dodging the traffic, he ran zigzag across the road, opened the taxi door, threw his rucksack onto the back seat, and slid the partition window open. 'Gunnersbury Station,' he told the driver. Then added foolishly. 'Got to meet someone off a train there.'

As the taxi drove off, he sank back in the seat, his heart pounding. Why had he told the taxi driver he was meeting someone off the train? That was stupid. The driver would wonder why his passenger wouldn't have gone from Ravenscourt Park on a train going to Richmond, which would be the quickest way to get to Gunnersbury. Which is what he should have done, instead of hailing a cab. He wasn't thinking straight.

At Gunnersbury, he handed the driver ten pounds, told him to keep the change, and then hurried into the station entrance, waiting until the taxi had gone before coming out. It took him another ten minutes to get his bearings and find her flat. Her car was nowhere to be seen, and he wondered if she had gone to pick him up and broken down or had an accident. It still didn't explain why her mobile wasn't working, and he felt the knot of foreboding tightening in the pit of his stomach as he climbed the stone steps to her front door. He couldn't see any lights on in the flat. Nothing but darkness and silence. If only he had argued with her about giving him a key. Now he had to rely on her turning up. But from where?

He rang the doorbell, and listened while it buzzed uselessly, summoning no one to the door. The flat was empty. He stood listening, straining for any sound. Nothing.

And then it occurred to him what might have happened. The stupid bitch drank too much. Maybe she had been stopped on the way to pick him up, failed a breathalyser test, and now well over the limit she was at the police station waiting for a police doctor to arrive to collect a blood sample. The stupid, stupid bitch!

The only thing to do now was collect his car, drive home, and somehow get rid of all the clothing, the rucksack, and the mobile phone. He would explain to Karen he needed to do some vital work in his study, which might take him all night. Then he could use his proper mobile to call Vanessa at her flat at odd intervals. Once she had given a blood sample they might let her go. He could then sneak back to her place, and the alibi might just hold.

But now the onus was on his wife to corroborate his story. There was only one way out of this mess now. He would have to tell Karen the truth.

As he drove towards Kew Bridge, he tugged the surgical gloves out the backpack which lay on the passenger seat, let the window down, made certain there were no cars behind him, then threw one of them out of the window. Further along Kew Gardens he threw the other one out.

He drove back through Richmond, and then through Petersham, which he thought was the most direct route home. To avoid being stopped by the police, he drove slowly and carefully, even though his mind raced with all his options, playing in his head the imaginary conversation he would have with Karen, trying to persuade her that he and Vanessa had done the right thing. She would take some convincing, and if Vanessa arrived home soon after he got to his place, then he would have to head straight back to Chiswick.

But as he thought about the essential alibi, he began to consider the possibility that the chances of anyone convicting him were slim. There was no evidence. As soon as he got rid of the clothing he had worn both before and during the crime, there was nothing. He had left no traces. He had watched many television crime dramas where the suspicions of the police were invariably aroused by a suspect with a perfect alibi, whereas a truly innocent person doesn't necessarily have an alibi. But that was television. Fiction. Even so, the lack of a perfect alibi might prove to be a blessing. If he and Vanessa were interviewed separately by the police, who knows how they might been tricked into given conflicting accounts of their apparent affair? He felt confident he could handle a police interview better on his own. That stupid bitch might put him right in it.

But Karen was the problem now.

As he drove past Petersham Common, he saw a row of shops on his right, and a small road running in front of them and parallel to the main road. Outside one of the shops was a garbage skip, which didn't look to be full, so he turned right into one of the streets near the shops, then turned left and stopped the car right opposite the skip, blocking the small narrow road. He had to be quick. It was still only 10.45, and someone coming back from a pub or cinema might see him. If that was the case, he would have to forget about getting rid of the rucksack and clothing, and find somewhere else to dispose of them. After he got out of the car, he stood for a moment looking up at the flat windows, just in case someone heard the noise from his engine and came to look out of the window. But everything in this short road was quiet, so he quickly opened the boot, took out the rucksack and dropped it into the skip. He leaned over, found a black bin liner full of rubbish, and placed it on top of the rucksack. Then he took off the baseball cap and threw it into a corner of the skip.

He got back in the car, and drove the short distance home, parking in the street instead of the underground car park, in case he needed to go out again. Either back to Vanessa's flat or to get rid of what he wore.

As soon as he walked into his flat, he sensed there was something very wrong. It was too quiet. Too quiet and too dark. He flicked the light switch in the hall and called Karen's name. Silence.

He went into the living room and paused, listening intently to the late-night sounds of the building, and the odd car going up Kingston Hill. It was nearly eleven o'clock. It wasn't like Karen to go out this late. Where the hell was she?

The biggest shock hit him like a battering ram when he went into the kitchen and discovered her note, propped against a crystal vase on the island work surface. His eyes scanned the message, brief and to the point.

Darling Paul,

Sorry, I didn't have time to cook you anything for when you get home, but I had to get to the airport quickly otherwise we would miss our flight. I hope you can manage for the next fortnight. See you in two weeks' time when Vanessa and I get back.

Love and kisses, Karen x

He felt bile rising in his throat and tears springing into his eyes just before the eruption. 'Fucking bitches,' he screamed as he picked up the

145

vase and hurled it across the kitchen. It hit the hob and smashed into tiny pieces.

As everything flashed through his brain like a speeded-up film, he realised just how he'd been conned, and knew exactly how they had done it.

Twenty

Vanessa saw the seat belt sign go off, and unclipped the buckle. Despite getting further into debt on one of her credit cards, she had no regrets about paying for two business class seats, which gave them more space to talk quietly and confidentially. She looked at her sister and smiled weakly as she whispered, 'Fingers crossed nothing went wrong and he managed to see it through.'

Karen wriggled as she struggled to unclip her seatbelt. 'When it comes to money, he's not the sort to back out. The shock will come when he knows he's on his own and might go to prison at last. I'd love to see his face when he realises his plan was shit.'

'Our plan,' Vanessa corrected her. 'Or should I say your plan? He only thought it was his plan – arrogant bastard – and now he'll pay the price for those other two "accidents" – she used her fingers as quotation marks – 'the killing of those two unfortunate women he got away with.'

'To think I was married to that cold-hearted bastard.'

'Was?' Vanessa questioned.

'Well, with any luck he'll get a life sentence. Then I'll have grounds to divorce him. Job done.'

They both lay back in their seats, staring ahead, imagining the horror of the crime and the outcome. After a long pause, Vanessa sat up and turned to look at her sister.

'After not speaking to me for five years, you contacted me on the day of Mummy's funeral. I haven't asked you: was this because you had begun to think about using your husband to—?'

'No,' Karen broke in. 'I just felt...I needed us to become friends again. I hadn't seen the private detective's report at that stage.' She sighed, wondering whether to tell her sister the truth about Paul hitting her, which may have been the catalyst in part of her decision to forgive Vanessa. Instead, she said, 'I think it was because Mummy wanted us to become friends again. And, I suppose, it was because I felt guilty that she passed away before it could happen. I wanted us to be pals again to honour her memory.'

Vanessa took her hand and squeezed it. 'I'm glad you did. And you have no regrets now, do you, about what we've done?'

'None at all.'

'I've never asked you this before. Did our father ever – I don't know how to put this – did he ever do anything to you when you were young?'

Karen, a distant look in her eyes as she remembered, shuddered before replying. 'I don't think I want to talk about it. What about you?'

Vanessa nodded. 'OK. Let's drop the subject, shall we?'

The drinks trolley arrived near their seats and a hostess asked them if they would like a drink before they ordered food. Karen asked for champagne to celebrate.

'D'you think that's appropriate?' Vanessa asked.

Karen relaxed and chuckled throatily. 'Oh, yes, I think so. It's not every day you feel you're on a journey to start over; the slate wiped clean.'

Vanessa grinned and turned to the hostess. 'Make that two champagnes, please.'

They sat quietly as they waited for the hostess to uncork the small champagne bottles. Karen thinking about the way she had engineered the plot soon after receiving the detective's report, which she had then sent to Vanessa, followed by clandestine meetings to work out the best way to get Paul hooked, with him all the while thinking it was his own master plan, never suspecting it was a plot to get rid of him as much as their father. The killing of two birds.

'What are you smiling at?' Vanessa asked.

'Was I smiling? I didn't realise I was. Maybe it's because I feel free for the first time in my life. Although I still miss Mummy terribly.'

'Yes, so do I. She was such a gentle person. You know, I don't think she'd approve of what we've done. In fact, she'd be mortified. Unless she knew about—' Vanessa stopped herself from mentioning it. Then added, 'They say it's therapeutic to talk about traumatic incidents in your past, but I don't agree.'

'No, neither do I. Especially now the future has changed for the better. Goodbye murky past, hello sunshine.'

The hostess handed them two glass flutes and champagne, then moved on along the aisle to the next row of seats. They raised their glasses to toast each other. 'New beginnings,' Vanessa said.

'Yes, new beginnings. I'll drink to that.'

After taking a sip, Vanessa giggled. 'After we became friends again, and you still had to convince Paul how much you hated me, I suppose you called me all sorts of names.'

'Only in general terms. I think fucking bitch may have escaped my lips a few times. And when you wrote me that letter, and I screwed it up, I saw the way Paul's crafty brain memorised your sandwich bar address as he straightened it out, pretending he admired your handwriting. I got a real buzz when I saw him taking the bait. What a gullible idiot.'

'What I find most incredible is the way he disposed of the Scottish wife, and then the widow in North Wales, and got away with it. Christ! A thought has just occurred to me. What if he gets away with it again?'

'How could he?'

'Well, when we were working out the details of the plot, he agreed that our father probably had many business enemies. Suppose – just supposing one of them has a strong motive and the police arrest the wrong person.'

'You're forgetting something. Once the body has been discovered, police will thoroughly search the Richmond house, and they'll probably come across that private detective's report in the study. That should make him the prime suspect. And if they get a search warrant for our flat, they'll find the copy of that report. Hidden in his office.'

'And you attached a computer printed note to it?'

'Yes, and I can remember the exact words I used. "Think you can get away with murder, do you? I'll destroy you like you destroyed your other two wives. And this is just the start. M Bradshaw." And they're not going to find my prints on that note. But why would they even think of fingerprinting it? Coupled with the detective's report, and the printed note from our father, it'll look like it came from him.'

'But that about the detective agency?'

'What about it?'

'You said one of them delivered the report to you personally.'

Karen shook her head. 'That doesn't matter. The report was printed on plain A4 paper. There is nothing to say which agency our father used to investigate Paul. Our father is the only person now who could tell the police where it came from. No, once the police read that report, all their investigations will be focused on Paul. They'll delve into his past to see if it's true.'

'And what if he confesses? It's me he'll drag down with him as his accomplice.'

'I've told you,' Karen said, sounding annoyed, 'several times. We just stick to the story. You only met Paul once, and that was five years back. He can hardly use you and say he was having an affair with you as an alibi. It just won't work. And the police, having read that report will know what a downright liar and manipulator he is.'

Vanessa sighed deeply. 'Yes, I'm sorry. It's just…I suppose I want some reassurance. I don't want anything to go wrong.'

'Don't worry. It won't. How the hell will Paul wriggle out of it? We bought the plane tickets a few weeks back. And we just stick to the story that he knew we were making this trip, especially after we became close again after all those years. Which is true. He's the only one who thinks we're still not speaking to each other. So, try not to worry. We've covered all the angles. You even put that small notice on the sandwich bar door last week saying it would be closed for a two-week holiday from today's date, didn't you?'

Vanessa nodded. 'Yes, and I even told Jason I was off to New York, and apologised for making him redundant. He already knew about my notice to quit the premises.'

'You see,' Karen said, 'there is no way my miserable husband will be able to deny knowing about us being friends again, or planning this trip, providing we both stick to the story. And there is no reason why we can't.'

Vanessa noticed tears in her sister's eyes, and saw her brush them away. 'What's wrong? Feelings of remorse?'

'Far from it. I was thinking about how happy I am now that we've become sisters again. Maybe we'll be closer now than we ever were.'

'And we've both spoken to Aunty Christine—'

'And she sounded over the moon about our reconciliation,' Karen jumped in, excitement in her voice. 'I can't wait to see her.'

'Me too. But—'

'But what? You're not having doubts, are you?

'Of course not. I love Aunty Christine. But she's a very perceptive person. Intelligent and bright. When the phone call comes – and it will – about our father's murder, how do we convince her we had nothing to do with it? It's what worries me more than anything else. I would hate it if she even suspected for a minute that we—'

Karen leant over, threw an arm across her sister's shoulders, and whispered, 'We can do it, Nessa, cos we love each other now. And we love Aunty Christine too. Try not to worry. I don't suppose the body will be discovered – well, at least not until tomorrow—'

'That's if he's managed to go through with it,' Vanessa said.

'Oh, believe me. As it involves money, and getting his film made, he'll do it all right. And after they discover the body, they'll want to inform us as his next of kin. But, as far as Aunty Christine is concerned, I will have already sown the bad seeds about Paul. When she asks how things are – which she's bound to do – I'll tell her about our father sending us that detective's report, and how I'm worried because I'm married to a suspected murderer. Don't forget, she heard the threats our father made during Mummy's funeral and that terrible scene.'

'You can't do that, Karen.'

'Why not?'

'Because you are supposed not to have seen that report. We worked out that our father sent it to your husband along with that threatening note. We've been through all this.'

'Yes, I know. Not that it matters. We can remind Aunty Christine about the way our father behaved at the funeral, and we plant the fact that Paul had a strong motive for killing him.'

'I shudder every time I think about Mummy's funeral and how he brought his little scrubber along.'

Karen removed her arm, leant back and finished her champagne. 'It's funny. If you hadn't seen them that time in Greenwich, we wouldn't have known about her being his mistress. He'd have got away with it.'

'I guess it was just meant to be then. Fate.'

'Because of the commotion, I didn't get a good look at her that day,' Karen said. 'I wonder what she's really like?'

'Who knows? And who cares? Just another young bimbo who thinks she's come into money. Now she can crawl back under that stone.'

Karen grinned and added, 'From whence she came.'

Twenty-one

On Saturday afternoon, as Melanie parked her Fiat outside the garage and saw the lights on in the house, she felt anxious. It was a sweltering hot day, cloudless and brilliant, so why would Marcus switch the lights on?

She walked carefully towards the front door, one hand placed firmly on her stomach, the other clutching the outrageously expensive handbag Marcus had bought for her thirty-second birthday, and then she stood for a moment, looking up at the fanlight, feeling nauseous. Was the sickly feeling because of her pregnancy, or because of something she had eaten recently? Or perhaps she was still tired after that exhausting week in Paris. A week watching her fiancé knocking back the wine, while she had to suffer strict obedience to her self-imposed prohibition.

Although she had a key to the house, she rang the bell, expecting to hear the familiar sound of her lover coming to let her in. She felt intimidated by the size and grandeur of the house and had never once used the key to let herself in. She was a stranger here, and suspected she always would be, knowing it was also *her* house, his wife's, even though she was dead now. She couldn't help feeling she was an interloper and an imposter, despite Marcus comforting her by generously offering to let her redesign and redecorate when she moved in.

As she waited, she heard children playing, their indignant cries carrying across the Green, and she thought about the tiny foetus inside her. The miracle, so small, growing to become like one of the children she could hear, screeching and shouting happily.

But where was Marcus? Why hadn't he come to open the door?

A cold trickle of fear snaked along her spine, and her breath caught in her chest. She sensed there was something very wrong, but tried to shake it off, trying to convince herself that her darling fiancé was probably in the shower, having worked late the night before; which was why he had given her a key. She was just being silly.

She placed the handbag on the front step, bent over, unzipped it and fumbled for the key. Where the hell had she put it? She wished now she had attached it to her own bunch of keys, instead of leaving it unattached to anything. After rummaging through the bag quickly, she found the key zipped in a side pocket, having forgotten she had put it in the compartment so that it could be easily located.

She slid the key into the lock and the door opened easily. The lights were on in the hall and on the stairway, and she could see lights shining from landing above. She closed the door behind her, and called out, 'Marcus darling. Are you home?'

As she moved to her left, she could see along the hall towards the kitchen. The horror of what she faced was like an icicle piercing her heart. She could see blood everywhere on the cream carpet, and Marcus lying in a pool of it.

Her mouth opened but her scream was a strangled rasp, her throat suddenly sandpaper raw with pain.

Her handbag fell to the floor and she froze, too scared to move. What if there was still someone else in the house? She tried to move but was too deeply shocked to do anything. The horror of what she saw was like a nightmare, and she felt helpless as tears burst into her eyes like a cataract, blurring her vision. She had to do something. *Call the police*. But she was petrified and still unable to move. Gradually, she inched forward, a little nearer to the corpse. Speeded up thoughts shot through her brain as voices wailed inside her, telling her she had lost everything now. Not only Marcus, but his fortune and her dream of opulence.

She was no longer solvent. She tried to push the guilty thoughts from her mind, but the inappropriate thoughts persisted while she desperately tried to mourn her lover. The shock was too great. It was hard to comprehend. This was someone else's nightmare.

As she stared at her lover's corpse, her eyes wide with terror, tears like a mist in front of her, it felt as if teeth were gnawing at her stomach, the pain increasing with every movement. Suddenly, the spasm hit her in the base of her stomach and she vomited copiously, coughing and spluttering. She pressed a hand against her stomach, praying her baby wasn't harmed by the shock to her system.

Her baby. And his baby.

Twenty-two

Although the murder made the late news on Saturday night, the reports were short on details, giving only sparse mention of a billionaire tycoon murdered in his West London home. But by late Saturday enough information was available to make the Sunday papers, and Marcus Bradshaw's name was revealed in all the media, with details of his marriage to the once famous model. And it was revealed that Melanie Martin, an actress, and the one who discovered the body, was his fiancée. Now the newspapers had been handed something more salacious and intriguing than a mere murder from an inept burglary, the juicy story could run to many editions for several weeks. If not longer.

Alice, stared at the headlines splashed across the front of the *Sunday Times* wondering whether to call Vanessa. She was torn between sympathy and a suspicion that her friend would not regret his death – would welcome it even. She remembered the conversation they'd had a few weeks back, when Vanessa seemed defensive about hating her father, protesting that she may have said it but not really meant it. There seemed to be something disingenuous about her protestation and Alice suspected her friend wasn't being entirely honest.

Alice knew Vanessa was in New York. Before leaving, Vanessa made a point of telling her how she and her sister had become reconciled immediately after the funeral. Which was most odd. There was that letter she was asked to post. That Saturday, weeks after the funeral, Alice called at her friend's flat and had was asked to post the letter to her sister. If the sisters were already reunited after the funeral, why had Vanessa said she was writing to plead for a reconciliation? It didn't make sense.

Although there was a niggling doubt in Alice's mind about Vanessa's honesty where her family was concerned, nevertheless she decided to give her friend the benefit of the doubt, and thought she may have got dates and days muddled up, seeing as she was under a great deal of pressure. No doubt she would soon be hearing all the gory details from her friend, over a few glasses of wine.

She decided to wait a few days before ringing Vanessa's mobile to offer her condolences. Although she was deeply sympathetic, because no one wants to lose a father in that gruesome manner, she couldn't help feeling intrigued and fascinated by the gripping real-life thriller in which she was involved, albeit on the periphery. Not everyone has a friend whose father has just been murdered, and Alice suspected there would be many family skeletons to emerge from the dark past of their history, and she couldn't wait to hear the rest of the story. After all, she was only human.

*

On Sunday afternoon Vanessa and Karen sat on folding directors' chairs on the balcony of their aunt's penthouse on Riverside Drive, staring at the view of the Hudson. They barely spoke as they waited for the dam to burst, the inevitable unfolding of the next instalment of their drama. They knew it was just a question of time before knowledge of the murder reached New York, and even if the US media didn't consider it worthy of much mention, surely their aunt would soon discover it on the internet, especially as she was a regular online reader of British newspapers.

Their aunt's husband, Richard, was a composer, and the sisters were relieved he was away in Hollywood scoring a film. As they hadn't seen him for over five years, they knew they would feel even more awkward about acting out the devastation of the bad news if he was around. They remembered how direct he was when he questioned anyone, almost as if anything he was told had to be analysed forensically.

The waiting was the worst part. Thankfully, their aunt was the only one they needed to convince that they had no prior knowledge of the crime, as her sons were out on dates with their girlfriends.

Vanessa sighed and stood up, leaning over the balcony, staring at the George Washington Bridge in the distance, with the sun glinting on the river, as she listened to the constant tyre-swishing sound of traffic on the Henry Hudson Parkway far below the building. Everything seemed unreal. Even the act of murder. It was not an event that bore any resemblance to their day-to-day lives. And yet, here they were, waiting for the crime to surface, to intrude on their calm exteriors. Her mobile phone lay on a small wooden table, and she desperately wished it would ring, to bring the fearful news that was expected at any time soon.

Their aunt offered them coffee, but they both declined, so she said she would leave them to it for a little while – as it was such a nice day, perhaps take them out later for a stroll through Central Park – but first she had one or two things to catch up with in her study. While they waited, silently wishing something would happen, they guessed she might go online and read the British newspapers. Fifteen silent minutes dragged by, the sisters staring at each other expectantly, saying not a word. Suddenly their aunt reappeared on the balcony and Vanessa almost jumped, with a startled intake of breath. It was her sister who remained calm, smiling as if nothing was amiss. Both had expected an emotional outburst from their aunt when she heard of the murder. Instead, she looked at them in turn, her face deadpan, taking her time before she spoke.

'I'm afraid I've got some bad news.' Another long pause. 'It's about your father.'

'What's happened?' Karen said.

'He's been murdered.'

Karin gasped. 'Murdered!'

'Someone shot him on Friday night. It's in all the papers.'

Vanessa opened her mouth wide, feigning shock and surprise; but Karen began wailing, keening like an actress in a Greek tragedy. Vanessa worried in case her sister went too far.

'I'm sorry,' their aunt said. 'I know you both fell out with him, but I don't think you would have wished that on him.'

Karen buried her head in her hands and sniffed loudly, disguising the fact that she couldn't produce any tears. Her aunt embraced her, and Karen managed to shudder convincingly. Vanessa stared at her aunt, and made a helpless gesture with her hands.

'I'm sorry,' she whispered. 'I just can't feel anything right now. Maybe I will when it hits me.'

'That's understandable. It's a terrible shock.'

'Do they know who—?' Vanessa began.

Her aunt shook her head, then gestured for Vanessa to come closer for a group hug. Karen felt her eyes smarting and watering slightly, and raised her head so that her aunt could see the glistening wetness, hoping it was enough to satisfy any doubts her aunt might have.

'It's terrible,' Karen sniffed as the three of them embraced. 'Much as I hated him, and he had cut us out of his life – he was still our father. Were there any…any details about the shooting?'

'That young woman – the one he said he was marrying – went round on Saturday morning and discovered the body.'

156

'God! That must have been awful for her. Who could have done such a thing?' Vanessa said. 'Oh, God, I feel…I feel so guilty.'

'Why should you feel guilty?'

'For attacking her the way I did at Mummy's funeral.'

'Nonsense. No one could blame you for that.'

Karen made a small choking noise, and hoped her performance was convincing. 'Aunty Christine, do you think we might have a brandy or something. I feel terrible. It might help calm my nerves.'

'Of course, why don't we all have one? I think we need it.'

When she returned with the three drinks, they all sat in the folding directors' chairs, sipping the brandy, staring at the New Jersey shore the other side of the river.

Eventually, their Aunt spoke. 'Karen, you mentioned threats your husband made towards your father.'

Karen nodded. 'He did. But only because he was scared.'

'You mean your father threatened Paul?'

'Yes, I think Paul was terrified of him.'

Vanessa's mobile phone, which was switched to vibrate, suddenly spun round on the smooth surface of the table as it buzzed. She froze.

'Aren't you going to answer it?' Karen prompted.

Vanessa picked it up, and her aunt and sister watched intently as they heard her tentative 'Hello?' Then she said, 'Yes, we've just heard the terrible news from my Aunty Christine here in New York. It's come as a terrible shock. Have you any idea who might have…No, of course not. Oh, yes, right. I see.' She made eye contact with her aunt as she spoke. 'I should think my sister and I could get an early flight tomorrow morning. Tonight? Well, we can try, but it might take some organising. We'll do everything we can to…I see.'

She stared at Karen. 'How long will he be helping you for? OK, we'll see if we can make a red-eye flight. We'll be there as soon as we can.'

She clicked the phone off.

'Who was that?' Karen asked.

'It was the Metropolitan Police. They want us to answer some questions about our father and…' she hesitated as she stared at Karen. 'And your husband, Karen. He's with them in custody.'

Karen faked an expression of agitation, her mouth opening and closing like a fish. 'They haven't arrested him?'

'No, they said he's helping them with their enquiries.'

'Hmm,' their aunt exclaimed. 'I don't want to upset you, Karen, but we all know what that means. I just hope for your sake he turns out to be innocent. But from what you told me about your father and your husband's feud—'

Karen put on her gravest expression, and managed to deliver a few small tears, although she really felt like punching the air jubilantly. As did her sister.

Twenty-three

After I got back to the flat that night, I suppose I panicked and wasn't thinking straight. I knew I had to get rid of the evidence, so I got a hammer and smashed the mobile phone to bits, first removing the SIM card. Then I changed out of the T-shirt, track-suit bottoms and trainers, shoved them into a plastic shopping bag, and went back out. It was only half-eleven and there were still quite a lot of people about. I walked towards Kingston town centre, getting rid of single items of evidence along the way, mainly in private wheelie bins in side streets. The SIM card I dropped down a drain. Big mistake. I should never have destroyed that mobile. If I'd kept it, Vanessa's text would still have been on it, and the police might have believed me about them setting me up. I suppose the crafty bitch guessed I'd get rid of it, and she wouldn't be implicated. There was nothing, absolutely nothing to show they were involved in a conspiracy to murder their father. I was well and truly fucked.

The first visit from the police was to inform Karen about the death of her father. When they asked me where my wife had gone, I was unable to tell them, and I could see this made them suspicious. That was on Saturday afternoon. On Sunday I was taken into custody, to answer questions under caution. They asked me again where my wife had gone and I said I thought they might have gone to New York, knowing they had an aunt who lived there. 'You mean you're not really sure where your wife went?' one of the cops said. I almost laughed as I watched them exchanging astonished expressions, performing like bad amateur actors. I thought they might opt for a good cop, bad cop interrogation, but there was none of that. They were always calm and polite. It was Detective Inspector Michael Tufnell who asked most of the questions, and I knew they had me bang to rights when they produced CCTV photographs showing my BMW in Richmond, going up past Richmond Bridge towards Petersham, at the approximate time of the victim's death. And a witness had come forward and described a man by the river behaving suspiciously, wearing a Nike baseball cap. They then told me they had found the baseball cap, and the backpack with the other clothes I wore, having retrieved them from the skip in Petersham. This evidence was with forensics, so they would no doubt find traces of my hair in the baseball cap. And that was just the start of it. They then produced a comprehensive report about Jenny's accident 15 years ago, and my murder trial for Donna's death, followed by my legal name change. That report came as an unexpected shock and I knew I hadn't a hope in hell of protesting my innocence. I mean, what was the point in lying anymore? I decided to confess, almost relieved it was over.

Over the next few days I made a thorough statement, determined to bring Vanessa down with me. The police told me the sisters had gone to visit their aunt in New York and they would be questioned as soon as they returned. But when they kept banging on about the detective agency report commissioned by my father-in-law, and I told them about the twins planning the crime to get rid of their father, my story and accusations began to sound far-fetched. I could tell they didn't believe me, and when they got around to interviewing those two bitches, I had to admit defeat and changed my statement, taking all the blame. Or all the credit, whichever way you look at it. Had I made that gangster film, I might have enjoyed my fifteen minutes of fame, but now my notoriety will last and people will remember this case for years.

No bail, of course. Just a long wait until the trial, with occasional visits from the solicitor. In my cell at nights, I used to fantasise about escaping from prison. It was a recurring daydream where I engineered a brilliant escape simply to take my revenge on those devious bitches from hell. It was always a slow death, with them pleading for their lives to be spared, or for death when the pain became too much for them to endure.

Maybe it would happen one day, I thought. That dream could become a reality, and I would have enough time on my hands to mastermind a foolproof plan to escape.

I was kept on remand until my trial at the Old Bailey in October. Why it took so long to come to trial I'll never know because the evidence against me was overwhelming. The CPS had a royal flush while I held nothing but a stacking hand. It was game, set and match to those two bitches. How could I have been so stupid? I should have realised something was brewing when Karen began playing the obedient wife.

My mother and father attended the trial, looking like grave and sullen statues, and sitting so close together I wondered if they were holding hands, but I could only see them from above the waist. Every so often I gave them a nice smile, but they didn't respond. Not a flicker of an eyelid. They probably hated me, their disloyal and only son shaming them. Well, that was tough, because there was no way I was going to sit through my trial and be anything but accommodating and pleasant. My biggest regret though was the position of the reporters to the dock. I knew some of them would be drawing an artist's impression of me, seeing as cameras are not allowed in a courtroom, and they would not be capturing me from my best side. Whenever I looked in a mirror I always thought I had a better profile on my right side, and the reporters were on my left. It was deeply regrettable but there was nothing I could do about it.

Another man who sat stony-faced in the gallery, staring at me with a glare of warning in his eyes, was Terry Lennox. Probably worried about being involved if the question arose of where I obtained a gun. I was already prepared for this one, and I had already made up my mind to lie. Perjure myself. I mean, what the hell did it matter? I could just say I went round some rough housing estates, made some enquiries, and then purchased it from someone who wanted to remain anonymous. And I had already sworn blind to my brief that this was the case. I don't know if he believed me, but frankly I didn't care.

And then that lie was shot to pieces when Karen gave evidence, talking about me needing money to make Lennox's film. She said she overheard me talking to him on the phone, asking him where I could get a shooter from. Presumably she'd read the term 'shooter' in Lennox's gangster script. Later, when my counsel cross-questioned her, he asked her why she hadn't been alarmed when she heard this in the phone call, and she answered that she thought it was something to do with a scene for the film.

Lying fucking bitch. I felt the smile freezing on my face, and when I looked up at Lennox he made a very subtle throat-slitting gesture. I knew then I'd have to watch my back wherever they sent me.

It was those sorts of distractions that ruined my concentration. It was my second murder trial and often my attention wandered as I preferred to study the expressions of the jurors and others in the courtroom, before being abruptly catapulted back into hearing sworn statements and evidence that could destroy me.

And it got worse, much worse as I saw my defence imploding. My defending counsel I soon realised was no match for the prosecution. When Karen was asked about the private detective's report that was sent by her father to me – the one I knew nothing about until I was in police custody – she denied knowing of its existence. She admitted knowing what it contained when she was interviewed by the police and they questioned her about it. She said the police told her it contained damning evidence about my murder trial in North Wales, and my first wife's accident in Aberdeenshire. She said if she had known what was in the report, she'd have been scared stiff, knowing she lived with a murderer.

That was when my counsel stood up and launched an objection at last, saying that I was acquitted of the crime, and the jury should not be influenced by that remark. The judge agreed and asked the witness to confine herself to answering the learned counsel's questions without making assumptions. She apologised, the judge asked the jury to ignore her remark, but the damage was done.

As I listened to Karen's testimony, I became aware of just how much she must hate me. She found a crafty way to crucify me with every question she answered, and in such an innocent-sounding way. She came across as naïve and trusting, and up until that point I hadn't realised just what a brilliant actor she was. And when I looked at the jury, I could see they were taken in by her performance.

When it was my counsel's turn to cross-question her, he asked her about my business going bust and her father being angered by the loss of half a million, and the time at her mother's wake when he threatened to come 'gunning' for me. I could see he was doing his best to impress the jury that Marcus Bradshaw was out to get me, and ended up by asking her if I seemed scared of him. I could see what he was doing, suggesting I was only trying to protect myself by getting to him first.

Compared to Karen's lengthy testimony, which lasted almost two hours, Vanessa spent only twenty minutes giving evidence about the threats her father had made at her mother's wake. I could see what the prosecuting counsel was doing, giving me yet another motive to kill her father. My barrister didn't even bother to question her. I couldn't really blame him; there didn't seem much point. I was well and truly shafted and I was going down for this crime. My only hope now was for damage limitation. And a key defence witness had yet to make an appearance. Luckily this came about from something Karen told me about her father not long after we were married.

First we heard from DI Tufnell, who gave evidence about the investigation, and then came the dog walker, who identified me as the man behaving strangely by the River Thames. Because I was now done up like a male model, wearing a smart, well-fitting suit, my barrister thought the dog-walker wouldn't be a reliable witness as he tried to identify the dapper man in the dock as the yob in the baseball cap. When he questioned the witness, he asked about his eyesight, and although the man admitted he wore varifocal glasses, he said he could see clearly and was satisfied that the man in the dock was the very same man he had seen at the edge of the river. I could see my barrister was trying desperately hard to discredit this witness, which I thought was a mistake. I saw by the expressions on the jurors' faces how this could have a negative impact on my defence.

When it was time for the key witness for the defence to make an appearance, I began to concentrate, knowing how the length of my sentence hung in the balance of her testimony. Linda Summerton was about fifty-years-old, with flowing blonde hair, and a pleasantly round face but with a slightly down swept mouth. Asked what her occupation was, she said she was unemployed, having been bankrupted four years ago, because of extreme intimidation from Marcus Bradshaw and his company. He had even gone to her private home and threatened her, after which she was terrified, especially as she received many threatening phone calls following this incident, and the climax came when she wouldn't budge on a deal, and Bradshaw followed her into a restaurant one day, grabbed her round the neck, then tipped her meal into her lap. There were many witnesses to this event, but she was so frightened of Marcus Bradshaw and his colleagues, she never made a complaint. But he pursued her in his business dealings right to the end, using every dirty trick at his disposal, until she went bust.

This evidence I guessed would damage Bradshaw's character, and I knew when I took the stand, no one would be able to prove he hadn't threatened me with violence.

When it was time for my questioning, my counsel relied heavily on this witness's testimony. Of course, I told some outrageous lies about Marcus Bradshaw, about him calling me to threaten grievous bodily harm, making certain his daughter wasn't around when he made those threats. I knew these lies couldn't be disproved so I thought I was on safe ground.

The prosecuting counsel tried to knock these into touch when he questioned me, but I stuck to my stories and gave a convincing performance.

The trial lasted just under three weeks and the jury reached a verdict in less than two hours. They found me guilty. No surprise there then. The court adjourned soon after and the sentencing would take place on the following day.

The court was packed for the sentencing. Looking up at the gallery I spotted my father-in-law's fiancée, her expression inscrutable, like she was attending a meeting about some sort of land regulation. I knew it was her because I'd seen her picture in the newspapers. I could see she was pregnant, and even though I faced prison, it cheered me up considerably knowing I'd robbed her of a potential goldmine for her bastard brat, and would have a miserable time of bringing it up.

The judge made his final preamble to the sentence, glossing over the fact that Bradshaw may have threatened me, which was no excuse, he said, for the heinous, premeditated murder for which there was no mitigation. I was sentenced to life with a recommendation that I serve no less than twenty-five years.

Just before the court was cleared and I was sent down, I looked up at Marcus Bradshaw's fiancée and smiled. It was my final act of revenge, knowing how my smile might torment her during her sleepless nights.

Twenty-four

Sitting at the long table in the dining hall, amidst the clatter of cutlery, and the smell of overcooked food, he swallows each mouthful without tasting it. The cells are overcrowded, and everyone on his table is disgusted not only by the food but the way there is now less time for leisure activities. More lock up time. He feels the pressure tightening at not only his table, but on every single table in the vast hall. There is such an extreme feeling of dissatisfaction and seething hatred, he feels he can almost touch it; taste it like the disgusting pig-swill food. And he wonders why the prison officers can't feel it like the inmates can. He senses there will soon be a riot with prisoners running amok, breaking up the place and getting rid of their pent-up frustrations. All the prisoners can sense it. It will take just one small loss of privilege, followed by a resentful argument, and the whole thing will blow sky high.

He uses his spoon to clear the last mouthful of lumpy mashed potato from his metal plate, and that's when he can feel the eyes through the back of his head. He wants to turn around, to see what his enemy looks like, but is suddenly very scared. He has seen this prisoner eyeing him up on several occasions, staring at him like a cat stalking a bird, but he could be wrong. Everyone in this high security wing looks threatening and evil.

Since his arrival here six weeks ago, he has attempted to use his smile to inveigle some of the inmates – those with a less intimidating demeanour – to join forces with him. Safety in numbers now will be his philosophy. Always a loner in the past, he must now surrender his independence and rely on the pack mentality, something he has always hated. Not only that, but for someone who has killed three times, he has a low threshold of pain, and suspects most of these hardened convicts can give or take a beating without any disproportionate sensation of pain.

But he can see they don't trust him. Whereas on the outside, in real life, everyone was deceived by his smile and believed in him. In here, they regard it with suspicion, so he tones it down, but the half-hearted grimace replacing it adds to the inmates' jaundiced opinion of him. In six weeks he hasn't found a single prisoner who likes him.

Picking up his tray, he slides his legs over the bench and turns around quickly. He catches the eye of the prisoner, who looks down at his meal. He knows he wasn't mistaken. He is being observed. And he knows that the convict is just biding his time, waiting for an opportunity.

As he carries his tray over to the tiered palette with the dirty metal crockery, he thinks about the prisoner who keeps him in his sights. Not exactly a bruiser. A wiry, timid-looking bloke with rodent features. More like a typical informer than a hardened villain. But then his expectations are coloured by what he's seen on television, and he is aware that some of the hardest villains or soldiers seldom look as if they are capable of extreme violence.

As he slides his tray into the palette, out of the corner of his eye he can feel rodent- face staring at him. He is about to walk away towards the stairs leading to his cell on the first floor when a commotion distracts him. He looks back and sees the wiry prisoner arguing with one of the screws, and he realises the riot is about to kick off, started by this prisoner.

Suddenly, tables are overturned. Clang and crash of metal. Splintering of wood. A siren, high pitched and piercing, wails across the jail, and the air is shaken by screams and shouts of anger and frustration.

He fights his way through a seething mass of prisoners, elbows digging into ribs, limbs flailing like semaphore signals. A knuckle lands on the side of his head, momentarily stunning him. It takes him a moment of disorientation to recover, and then he fights his way through a throng of rampaging convicts, heading towards the stairs and the safety of his cell. If he can convince the screws he wants out of this riot, show them he means to seek sanctuary in his cell, he might survive the mob's violent behaviour.

He reaches the stairs, but two screws with truncheons and riot shields are hurtling down towards him. He clutches the banister, turning away from them, showing them he wants no part of this frenzied violence. They clatter past him, intent on dealing with the rampaging mob in the hall below. He hurries to the top of the stairs. More screws are running along the passageway past his cell. He waits at the corner at the top of the stairs, lets them hurtle past him, then dashes along the catwalk to his cell, pushes open the door and enters. He is about to exhale, when his breath stops, and a cold wind of fear gusts through his body, and in his head he hears a macabre warning cry.

There are two of them waiting in his cell and he doesn't stand a chance. One of them knocks him to the floor and there's a loud crack as his head

166

hits the edge of the bunk bed. Something slips over his head, across his face. It feels like a wire. He tries to slip his fingers in between the wire and his neck, but it's being pulled too tight. He struggles and fights for breath, but the wire cutting into his neck is too painful and he can't breathe. Faces from his past stare at him accusingly as he struggles to suck in air, his lungs about to burst. The wire cuts into his neck. No breath left. The pain is in his chest. The pressure building, his lungs about to explode. Darkness comes swiftly. Pitch black. And then, nothing.

Twenty-five

The excitement of the television presenters grated on Melanie, and the Christmas songs got on her nerves. It was almost time for the one o'clock news, so she switched off the television just as the BBC News theme started. She found the news too depressing. Death and destruction everywhere, a reminder of her own loss.

She struggled to get up off the sofa, thinking she might tidy her flat. The living room needed a thorough clean, and there was a stale smell in the air. She wondered if it came from her tiny bedroom, where there was barely enough room in the built-in wardrobe to hang all her clothes. And hardly any shelf space, which meant her clothes, both clean and dirty, tended to get flung in a great pile over a chair.

Hoping the smell would disappear, she shut the bedroom door, then patted her stomach, wondering how she would cope with being a single mother. It was the last week in November, and the baby was due in less than two months' time. She knew her mother and father would moan and groan about the upheaval, having to make the journey from Winchester so they could be with her when she gave birth. But what irritated her far more was their silent disapproval, the way they shook their heads in unison, as they did when she told them back in June she intended marrying a man of fifty-nine.

Distracting herself from negative thoughts, she went into the small galley kitchen at the back of the flat, and switched the kettle on. She was just about to drop a camomile tea bag into a cup when the doorbell rang.

She wasn't expecting anyone. Most of her friends sent a text before calling. It was probably a cold sales call, so she sighed before going out into the communal hall, hoping her pregnancy and a severe expression might drive away any cold callers or religious freaks. She threw open the front door, and stepped back in alarm as the blast of cold air hit her. But it wasn't the temperature that took her breath away. It was seeing them. His daughters.

'I know this must come as a shock,' Karen said. 'But if we phoned first—'

'You might have said you didn't want to see us,' Vanessa added. 'And I know this is totally unexpected, but we have a very good reason for wanting to see you.'

Karen saw Melanie shivering from the bitter temperature and smiled. 'It's freezing out here. And I don't know much about pregnancy but…can we come in and talk to you?'

Melanie's first instinct had been to shut the door in their faces, but her curiosity was aroused, and she was intrigued to know what they wanted. Besides, what did she have to lose by inviting them in to hear what they had to say?

She stood aside, allowing them to enter, and said, 'Please ignore the mess in the flat. I haven't had a chance to—'

Karen smiled and waved it aside. 'Not to worry. I'm sure all your time's taken up with keeping yourself healthy for the birth.'

'Hardly,' Melanie giggled. Then became serious as she closed both doors and ushered them into the living room. 'Why have you suddenly come to see me?'

They both hovered awkwardly in the centre of the room as Karen said, 'I know I apologised to you when I met you outside the court last month, after Paul was sentenced. I felt guilty because I was married to him. How could I, or anyone else, have been taken in by him?'

Melanie held both arms around her stomach, as if protecting her baby from harmful emotions. 'At least he won't come out for twenty-five years. Thank God!' She noticed a look that passed between the sisters. 'What's wrong?'

'You mean you haven't heard?'

'Heard what?'

'It was on yesterday's news. He's dead. There was a riot in the prison and someone murdered him.'

'I'm sorry, Karen. I really am.'

'Don't be. I won't mourn his loss. I think it was worse when I discovered I was married to a murderer.'

Melanie looked up, tears trickling down her cheeks as she mumbled, 'You weren't to know.' She sniffed, brushed the tears away with her fingers, and wiped her hands on her floral smock. 'And it can't have been easy for you – either of you – losing your father like that. Oh, I know he wasn't speaking to you, but I kept telling him to forgive you. And given

169

time we all might—' She stopped, and looked wistfully into the distance. 'But I guess it's too late now.'

'Perhaps not,' Karen said, 'because…'

'We have a proposition to put to you,' Vanessa finished. 'Do you mind if we all sit down?'

Melanie nodded. 'We could sit at the dining room table. Those are the only chairs with no rubbish on them. I'm sorry, I hate normal tea and coffee now, and I've had no visitors lately, so all I can offer is camomile tea.'

'I'm fine,' Karen said, with a wave of her hand as she sat down.

'Me too,' Vanessa said.

After the three of them had sat at the table, there was an awkward silence, which Karen was the first to break as she opened her handbag. 'Your baby – do you know yet…'

'What sex it will be?' Vanessa said.

'It will either be our baby brother…'

'Or baby sister.'

Noticing the sisters finishing each other's sentences, Melanie wondered if this was typical of twins.

'I know it will be our half brother or sister, but—'

Melanie waited for Vanessa to end the sentence, but she remained silent. Karen pushed a piece of paper across the table towards her. Melanie's eyes widened when she saw the Lloyds Bank name and emblem at the corner, and realised it was a cheque.

'This is for you to provide for your baby,' Vanessa said, exchanging a smile with her sister, who added, 'And to buy a house or flat in a decent district.'

Melanie's voice was hoarse as she stared at the amount on the cheque. 'This is for half a million pounds.'

Vanessa laughed. 'Yes, well, it doesn't get you very much in the way property these days.'

'And I know we can afford a great deal more,' Karen said. 'But we said we have a proposition for you. We're going to set up a charitable foundation, an agency to protect children. And we would like to offer you a place to work alongside us. How do you feel about that, Melanie?'

'Well, that's fantastic, but I've no experience of—'

Vanessa brushed it aside with a shake of the head. 'It doesn't matter. None of us have, but we can soon learn. And we can buy expert advice.'

'I don't know what to say. This is fantastic, coming out of the blue like this. Especially as it's come at such a depressing time, so soon after that trial. Although getting nearer the day of the birth has managed to keep me sane.'

'And talking of sanity,' Karen said, 'let's discuss the future of our brother or sister—'

'Brother,' Melanie cut in. 'I've had several scans, and he is definitely a boy.'

'Well, we would like to be good sisters to our baby brother – like godparents. But we would like him to grow up unspoilt. Although we can afford to give him a good private education, we'd prefer him to attend a state school.'

'In a good district, of course,' Vanessa specified. 'Somewhere like Teddington or Hampton. And then, perhaps, with you as his mother, and us as his loving sisters, between us we can bring him up to be a good man. Someone who will change the world.'

Smiling at Melanie, Karen added, 'For the better. Although he will always be able to fall back on the help of his big sisters, we would like him to become self-sufficient. Not having to rely on a rich family to get him out of trouble. Who knows? Maybe when he's older, he might want to run our children's charity.'

Vanessa glanced at her sister. This was the nearest they would ever come to their redemption and they knew it. 'You can't change the past,' she quoted, 'but you can change the future.'

Karen nodded. 'And with the three of us bringing him up, he'll have a good chance of becoming the future. A good person.'

She wanted to add, not like our father, but stopped herself.

'But mainly,' Vanessa said, 'we won't bring him up to be rich and spoilt. He'll be independent. Make his own way in the world. After all, there's no gain without pain.'

Realising what she had said, Vanessa's intake of breath was loud as she threw an expression of alarm in Karen's direction. But, like the rumble of an earthquake, her sister snorted, tried to stop herself from laughing, then submitted to a full-throated roar as she saw the funny side of her sister's faux pas.

Melanie was nonplussed as she saw the twins laughing uncontrollably, tears of laughter streaming down their faces, and she wondered just what was so funny.

For Vanessa and Karen this was a healing process bringing them closer together. Now they were a family again, and could move on.

About the Author

David Barry has been an actor for more than fifty years having started as a child actor when he attended Corona Academy Stage School. His first professional appearance was in Life With Father at Windsor Theatre Royal. Aged 14 he toured Europe in Titus Andronicus with Laurence Olivier and Vivien Leigh. His first film was Abandon Ship with Tyrone Power and Mai Zetterling, and he also appeared in the Walt Disney version of The Prince and The Pauper. In his early twenties he played Frankie Abbott in the television sitcoms Please Sir! and Fenn Street Gang and also appeared in the film of Please Sir! He played Elvis, Stratford John's nephew in George and Mildred the Movie. He wrote an episode of Fenn Street Gang and also contributed scripts for Thames Television's Keep It in The Family.

He has appeared in countless television productions including The Bill, Never the Twain and A Mind to Kill. And in the theatre he has performed in The Creeper, The Taming of The Shrew, Funny Money, Under Milk Wood and dozens of pantomimes in which he has played many characters from Buttons to Dame.

His first novel Each Man Kills was published in 2002, and republished in 2014 by Andrews UK, who also published some of his other novels including Willie the Actor, A Deadly Diversion, Careless Talk and More Careless Talk. They also published his children's book The Ice Cream Time Machine and his collection of short stories Tales from Soho.

In 2011 Hale Books published in hardback his historical novel Mr Micawber Down Under which he later adapted into a play, now published by Lazy Bee Scripts, and in 2015 he wrote A Day in The Lives of Frankie Abbott in which he revived his sitcom character as a 70-year-old resident in a care home, and this was produced by Misty Moon, touring the south east followed by a production at the Edinburgh Fringe Festival 2016.

He is also a radio presenter and broadcasts a music and chat show weekly on Channel Radio. He lives in Tunbridge Wells and has two grown up children.

www.davidbarryauthor.co.uk

www.twitter.com/dbarrywriter

www.facebook.com/david.barry

Lightning Source UK Ltd.
Milton Keynes UK
UKHW011004111219
355179UK00001B/66/P

9 781999 327705